I0817961

DON'T REMEMBER

(A Taylor Sage FBI Suspense Thriller—Book 5)

Molly Black

Molly Black

Bestselling author Molly Black is author of the MAYA GRAY FBI suspense thriller series, comprising nine books (and counting); of the RYLIE WOLF FBI suspense thriller series, comprising six books (and counting); of the TAYLOR SAGE FBI suspense thriller series, comprising six books (and counting); and of the KATIE WINTER FBI suspense thriller series, comprising nine books (and counting).

An avid reader and lifelong fan of the mystery and thriller genres, Molly loves to hear from you, so please feel free to visit www.mollyblackauthor.com to learn more and stay in touch.

ISBN: 978-1-0943-9546-3

BOOKS BY MOLLY BLACK

MAYA GRAY MYSTERY SERIES
GIRL ONE: MURDER (Book #1)
GIRL TWO: TAKEN (Book #2)
GIRL THREE: TRAPPED (Book #3)
GIRL FOUR: LURED (Book #4)
GIRL FIVE: BOUND (Book #5)
GIRL SIX: FORSAKEN (Book #6)
GIRL SEVEN: CRAVED (Book #7)
GIRL EIGHT: HUNTED (Book #8)
GIRL NINE: GONE (Book #9)

RYLIE WOLF FBI SUSPENSE THRILLER
FOUND YOU (Book #1)
CAUGHT YOU (Book #2)
SEE YOU (Book #3)
WANT YOU (Book #4)
TAKE YOU (Book #5)
DARE YOU (Book #6)

TAYLOR SAGE FBI SUSPENSE THRILLER
DON'T LOOK (Book #1)
DON'T BREATHE (Book #2)
DON'T RUN (Book #3)
DON'T FLINCH (Book #4)
DON'T REMEMBER (Book #5)
DON'T TELL (Book #6)

KATIE WINTER FBI SUSPENSE THRILLER
SAVE ME (Book #1)
REACH ME (Book #2)
HIDE ME (Book #3)
BELIEVE ME (Book #4)
HELP ME (Book #5)
FORGET ME (Book #6)
HOLD ME (Book #7)
PROTECT ME (Book #8)
REMEMBER ME (Book #9)

PROLOGUE

Every moment in Special Agent Taylor Sage's life had come down to this.

The old, weathered cabin door swung open in front of her. A gust of cold, musty air filled her nose. The floorboards creaked beneath her feet as she took an uneasy step inside, her heart pounding violently in her throat.

If Taylor was right, then Angie—her sister, who vanished without a trace twenty years ago—could be here, in this cabin. She'd found the symbol from the tarot reader's prediction, and now she was here. Ready to face whatever came next.

Taylor found herself standing in a dingy room with a broken window. The floor was covered in a thin layer of dust and grime, and the air was thick with the smell of mold and mildew. The window was cracked, and the glass was missing in several places. There was a table in the middle of the room, and a chair was overturned next to it. The room was empty.

There was no sign of life.

Taylor's chest had never been tighter. *Breathe, Sage. Breathe.*

She took another step forward. There were no visible signs of life—but Taylor couldn't shake the spine-tingling feeling that she wasn't alone.

That she was being watched.

Taylor drew in a sharp breath and spun around suddenly, facing the door. Nothing. The air was still.

She was just being paranoid.

Sighing softly, she turned back around.

Less than four feet away, the back wall of the cabin came into sight. The wall was lined with cabinets. Taylor's throat went dry. She crept toward the cabinets and placed a shaking hand on the door handle of one of them. Her throat tightened, and her head spun as she pulled the door open.

The cabinet was filled with decades of dust and cobwebs. Inside were only a few cans of food, a box of matches, and a few tattered magazines.

Taylor's hands trembled as she closed the cabinet. She looked inside the rest of them with the same result.

There was nothing here. Taylor hadn't found Angie.

A sense of frustration flooded Taylor's chest. She clenched her fists in frustration. Why was she wasting her time at the cabin when she could be out there, searching for Angie? Was this really the wrong spot? It made no sense; the symbol had brought her here. There was no way all of that was just a coincidence.

"Where are you, Angie?"

Taylor's chest tightened. If Angie was gone, then they could never be a family again. All of this really would be for nothing. The tarot cards, the symbol, this wild goose chase… Taylor felt like she was going crazy. Maybe she'd dreamt all of this up, and it was just one very long nightmare.

But no. She was here, in this moment, and the symbol—it had been real. She had to keep looking.

Taylor turned her attention to the small kitchen in the back corner. The sink probably hadn't worked in years. But as Taylor looked around the dusty countertops, something gleamed in the moonlight. She drew closer.

It was a fork.

And on it was what looked like fresh tomato sauce.

Her heart thudded as she looked closer. In the sink was an open can of ravioli. Fresh. So fresh Taylor could still smell the tomatoes and spices.

Someone was here.

Taylor whipped around, just as—

Taylor sensed something coming right for her.

The sound of the air whipping as something was thrown across the room filled Taylor's ears. Ceramic shattered against the wall. She ducked down and spun to face her assailant.

It was a man.

A crazed, decrepit, older man. He had white hair and dark, piercing eyes. His skin was wrinkled and weatherworn, and he was dressed in torn, tattered clothes that were once probably a bright and colorful plaid.

The old man smiled at Taylor with a mouthful of yellow teeth and reached for her. Taylor stalked backwards, but the old man matched her every step, his hands outstretched, his smile growing wider.

"You!" he yelled.

Taylor stilled. Something about his voice was familiar.

The old man stepped closer, and Taylor could see the outline of his thin, hunched figure in the moonlight. Her brow furrowed as she looked closer. She recognized the face—but from where?

It didn't matter. Maybe he was someone from their past. Taylor didn't care. In that moment, all she cared about was knowing if Angie was still alive.

"Where the hell is my sister?" Taylor demanded.

The old man spat. "Damn you. You ruined everything," he growled.

"You're the one who took Angie," Taylor hissed. She had no proof yet—but inside, she knew it was true.

There was a pause as the old man glared at her.

Then he smiled.

"You think everything is so black and white, don't you?" He laughed, a hysterical, wheezing laugh. "It's so much more complicated than that, my dear."

"Where is she?" Taylor demanded. There was a pause.

"I don't know," the old man said.

"You're lying!" Taylor said, approaching him. "You took her!"

"I didn't," he said.

Taylor's blood boiled. "You're the only one who knows where she is!" she yelled. "Tell me where she is!"

"No," he said.

Taylor's hands balled into fists. She could feel her hair standing on end.

Then he said: "I won't let you have her."

Taylor's resolve burned to life. Every fleeting hope, every delusion, every dream she'd had over the past twenty years all suddenly felt within arm's reach.

This son of a bitch really did have Angie.

Anger flushed through her entire body, like a sheet of lightning. She would not let this man stand between her and Angie. With a sudden burst of energy, Taylor lashed out. She grabbed the old man by the collar of his shirt, yanked him up off his feet, and slammed him against the wall.

"Where is she?" Taylor demanded again.

He merely smiled, showing off his yellow teeth. "I already said I don't know," he hissed.

Taylor felt the rage surge within her. She slammed the man against the wall again. "Tell me where she is," she said.

"You're a fool," he said.

Taylor's body began to shake with rage. "Tell me where she is," she said, her voice cracking with intensity.

The old man chuckled. "You can't have her. She's mine."

She didn't have time for this anymore. Taylor stood back and whipped out her gun, pointing it right at his face.

"Tell me where my sister is or you die."

She wouldn't shoot him, not to kill—Taylor didn't want him dead. She wanted answers. Who was he? Why was he so familiar? And why did he take Angie? He deserved to rot in a cell—but it didn't hurt to let him think Taylor would really blow his brains out.

But he just smiled at the barrel of the gun.

"She's mine," he said. "She loves me. She's loved me all this time. You can't keep us apart."

Something audibly clicked.

And before Taylor had a chance to process it, he had his own handgun out. But he didn't point it at Taylor—he just held it limply in his hand.

"Drop that," Taylor demanded. "Now. Drop it."

But his arm limply raised the gun up, and up—until it was pointed right at his head.

No! Taylor threatened him with her own gun again, as if that would make him stop. "Drop the weapon now," Taylor said. "Do not shoot."

"She loves me," the old man said. "She loves me, and she chose me… you can't take her away. You can't. Then I'd be all alone…"

"Drop your weapon, now!" Taylor said.

"She loves me so much that she ran away from home to be with me," the man said.

"Drop your weapon," Taylor said. She couldn't—wouldn't—listen to a single thing this man had to say. Angie didn't run away. He stole her. Taylor wouldn't believe anything else.

"Who's going to love her now? Who's going to take care of her? Who's going to cook for her?" The man lifted the gun higher.

"Stop it!" Taylor said. She raised her gun more. She didn't know what to do. Shoot his leg? His arm? She had to stop him, but—

The man's finger curled around the trigger.

"Stop!" Taylor said.

The old man stared at Taylor. His eyes were dark, and they were suddenly brimming with tears.

"No," he whispered.

Taylor's heart was torn. "Drop the weapon," she said, her voice cracking. Desperation took hold of her. She just needed the truth. If he killed himself, she might never get it.

The man stared at her, terrified. He was shaking with fear. "I don't want to live without her, ever," he whispered.

"Don't do this," Taylor whispered.

"Please," he said again, his voice cracking. He was begging her. "Don't make me do this. She'll die without me. She loves me."

Taylor's stomach rolled. She wanted to throw up.

"Don't," she warned him again.

The old man closed his eyes.

"No!" Taylor screamed. She dove in, trying to grab his weapon—but it was too late.

He fired.

The sound of the gun pierced Taylor's ears. She froze. She couldn't move. Couldn't breathe. Her eyes went wide and her mouth hung open as she watched the man's body fall to the floor.

A hole in his head was oozing blood onto the carpet.

She was too stunned to move. She just stood there, staring at the body.

What have I done?

How did she let this happen? Why didn't she shoot? Taylor didn't know. She had been petrified, physically and mentally. She'd frozen.

But she couldn't freeze up anymore. She was too close. Finally, she snapped out of it. Her brow furrowed, and her eyes narrowed. She rushed over to the old man. Tears welled up in her eyes as she knelt down beside him. The wound continued to spill blood, and his eyes were glassy as he stared at nothing.

He was dead.

"Damn you," she whispered. "Damn you to hell."

Taylor wanted to cry. She wanted to scream. She wanted to puke.

But the sound of something shuffling somewhere in the cabin filled Taylor with a sudden panic. She whipped around, too fast, and the world began to spin. Her head ached. Her stomach churned.

Taylor could barely see. She felt like she was going to vomit.

"Angie!" Taylor cried out. "Are you in here?"

She had to keep looking. She couldn't give up.

She dove into the bedroom of the cabin. There was nothing there but a shabby bed, a dresser, and a bookshelf, plus a single stream of moonlight through the window. The man must have slept here.

The shuffling sound again. Taylor spun around.

Something else—or somebody else—was in here, somewhere, but she didn't know where. *Please be Angie. Please be Angie…*

The sound came again—something metallic, something moving. It sounded like it was coming from behind the bookshelf. Without thinking, Taylor threw the bookshelf down, letting its old, rotting wood splinter against the floor.

Behind the bookshelf was a small door.

Taylor's heart leapt into her throat.

"Angie! Angie!"

No response came. But she heard the rattle of what sounded like chains being dragged across a floor. Taylor grabbed the knob of the door and twisted.

Locked.

"Damn it," Taylor said. She didn't have the right tools to break down the door. She turned back to the body of the dead man through the doorway. She'd been in such a panic before that she didn't even see the keys on his belt.

"I didn't want you dead," she muttered to the body. "You should have just told me. You should have just told me the truth."

She knelt back down. The body's eyes were still open, staring up at the ceiling. She thought about closing them, but she couldn't bring herself to touch him. To touch the man who'd kept her sister captive for all these years.

The keys jingled in her hand. She grabbed them and ran back into the bedroom, then slipped a key into the door, twisted it, and turned the knob.

It opened.

Taylor heard the sound again. The rattling.

But beyond the door was just a dark, empty closet…

Or so it appeared.

Taylor stepped inside. The chain rattled again. It was coming from behind one of these walls. Taylor knocked on them. The walls seemed hollow, like they were just pieces of plywood stacked on top of one another. Taylor don't know where Angie was, but she'd have to look through all of these walls.

She kicked one of them in, surprised by how easily her foot went through. It wasn't a wall. It was just cardboard. Taylor tore through it until she reached a room on the other side.

And inside, in a small, cramped crawlspace, was a woman, chained to the back of the wall. Hunched in the corner, wearing rags. Long, black hair. Unrecognizable. Emaciated.

But when she looked at Taylor, Taylor saw those blue-gray eyes, haunted as they were, and Taylor knew.

It was Angie.

CHAPTER ONE

Working at the flower store had been a dream of Mary's since she was a child, and now, she was old enough to really do it. Not only that, but at only twenty-six years old, she'd saved enough money to—with the help of her parents, of course—open her own store.

It was dark outside, and Mary smiled to herself as she closed up the shop, stepping into the cool night. She turned the key in the lock, ready to go home for the night. First, she gazed inside the windows at her shop, at all the flowers and pottery. The store was dark, the moonlight casting a cold, pearlescent light on each individual item: the baskets and bins, the light fixtures, the shrubs and the potted plants, everything that existed within the confines of these windows. Mary was proud to call this hers. And she'd worked hard for it.

Breathing in a breath of nighttime air, Mary turned away from the store. The only thing that really bothered her about this location was that there was never any parking available on the road, and her shop didn't have its own lot, so Mary often ended up having to park way up the street.

Still, she was lucky she had a car, and it was paid off at that. Mary loved to count the little things in life. If she kept up a positive attitude, then everything would work out.

She started walking, pulling her coat shut as the early autumn wind chilled her. The cars parked up and down the road were few and far between at this hour. Mary could hear the sound of her feet thudding against the pavement. It was cold, but it wasn't too bad… Mary always tried to look on the bright side.

She shivered as the wind picked up. She pulled her coat tighter, the wind blowing through it, but she was almost at her car. Just a bit farther. When she got home, she planned on watching her favorite sitcom with a tub of ice cream. Maybe she'd draw a bath. Maybe bake some cookies, although her parents hated it when she stunk up the house so late, even with the fresh, delicious scent of baked goods.

As Mary passed by a building, she looked up at its sign. A clown face with a big smile looked down on her. Mary didn't like to be mean, but this place always gave her the creeps. Through the windows she could see the walls of toys and dolls. She would have loved it as a little girl, but these days all Mary really cared about were flowers.

But as Mary was passing by the building, she heard a sound. No—it was a voice. High-pitched, almost childlike…

"Help…"

Mary's heart fell. Was she hearing things? It was late. There was no way a child would be out at this hour.

Mary shook her head and kept walking. She must have imagined it. *Don't be so silly.*

The high-pitched voice called out again, this time unmistakably. "Help…"

Mary turned around and stared up at the building. The voice came from beside the building, in the alleyway, she was sure of it. She took a few steps toward the building.

"Help me…" came the voice again, and then a small, pained cry.

Mary stopped. Somebody was in that alleyway. That was for sure. And they sounded young. At the very least, they sounded like a child. Her stomach fell as she was thinking this was every parent's nightmare. Their child getting lost in the dark, calling out for help. Maybe they were hurt. But the alleyway looked long and dark, and truthfully, it gave Mary chills. A bad feeling roiled inside of her.

But it was the right thing to do, wasn't it? Go into a potentially dangerous alleyway to save a child? Mary would normally not put herself in a dangerous situation, but this child—they could really need help. What if they died and Mary could have saved them?

It was decided, then and there. She had to help.

"Help me…"

Mary took a step into the dark alley. "Hello? Is anyone there? Are you hurt?"

Her heart stalled. It was so dark, she could barely see. She squinted and looked down the alleyway. There was a dumpster and some trash cans, and a fire escape on the wall in the distance. The trash cans were all shapes and sizes, but she couldn't see anything else. She couldn't see a small child. And she certainly couldn't hear anything over the sound of her own heart pounding in her throat. *Maybe this was a bad idea…*

Mary stepped forward, her hand brushing the rough brick wall of the building.

"Hello?" she called out.

There was no answer, just the sound of her shoes on the asphalt.

“Is anybody there?” she called out.

“Help…” came the small voice, and Mary’s heart stopped. She had heard it. There was no doubt about it. And it came from the alleyway.

Mary stepped forward, her hand groping for something. Anything. It collided with the trash cans. She pushed them out of the way until she found the wall again.

Moonlight snuck between the buildings. Mary’s vision began to adjust to the lack of light, slowly, but surely.

“Help me…”

And then Mary saw it. A small, pale shape. She ran forward, dropping her bag to the ground. She couldn’t tell what it was in the darkness, but it didn’t look right.

Mary got closer.

And it came into view. A small, pale porcelain doll. It had black hair in ringlets, a frilly white dress, black-painted lips, and glassy eyes. *What the…?*

“Help me…”

Was the voice coming from the doll? This didn’t make sense, but Mary was thoroughly creeped out. It definitely sounded like it was coming from in front of her. She reached down, her fingers clenching the doll’s shoulder. It felt cold to the touch, and the hard porcelain felt more like metal.

Mary’s mouth hung open. She’d never seen anything like this. It was so creepy. She would have taken one more step back, but at that moment the moonlight snuck out from behind the clouds and shone directly on the doll.

Mary froze as she looked into the doll’s eyes.

Then the voice again: “Oh, you came to help me…”

But the voice wasn’t coming from the doll at all.

It was coming from behind her.

She froze in place. She felt somebody’s hot, sick breath on her neck.

Then something yanked back hard on her hair, hurting her scalp.

Mary screamed. And at that moment, she knew she’d made the worst mistake of her life.

CHAPTER TWO

Taylor paced the hospital hallway, feeling like she was going insane. The hallway was white and clean and much too sterile for comfort. She felt as though she was trapped inside a corpse, unsure of whether the air was poison. The rhythm of her steps drifted in time to some faint tune playing in a distant room.

Angie was back.

Taylor's sister, who had gone missing two decades ago, had been found. But they wouldn't even let Taylor see her—Angie was still being treated by the doctors, and every moment that passed made Taylor want to bite her nails off. *Come on, let me see her!*

Taylor hadn't slept, not since Angie was found. When Taylor got into the room Angie had been kept in, Angie had lost consciousness, maybe out of shock. Surely, after being held captive by that man for so many years, Angie had never expected to see Taylor's face again.

Every moment since then had been a whirlwind. All Taylor wanted was to hear her sister's voice. To have a conversation with her. To catch her up on all the years she'd missed. To tell her how she'd never given up on the hope that Angie was alive.

Dealing with the crime scene had been a mess. Officers had come to the cabin, and Taylor had to explain everything—how she'd found the place, who Angie was, and why the perpetrator was now dead.

It took hours. Angie had been taken to a hospital. After that, Taylor had been questioned over and over again by the police, by the FBI, and by everyone in between. But no matter how many times she was asked, Taylor never told them anything other than what she'd told the officers who'd come to the cabin. Taylor was forced to leave the policework to them, as it was in their jurisdiction. But Winchester had taken over on the FBI front and sent Taylor away to the hospital. Taylor had a certain privilege being with the FBI, and Winchester had come in to help deal with the whole thing. Her partner, Wesley, however, still hadn't answered Taylor's text—she'd sent him one just before going into the cabin. But it was late. He was probably asleep.

That brought her here, to this hospital. Over and over again, Taylor asked them if she could see Angie. But every time, they told her the same thing—that Angie was unconscious, and they didn't know when she'd wake up. They wouldn't let her see Angie. But she was alive, and she was right behind that door. Taylor's parents were on their way, and she knew they'd raise hell to see her when they got here.

It all still felt like a dream.

Taylor had spent so many years wishing her sister were somehow still alive. All the dreams, all the signs the tarot cards pointed to—they were all right.

Angie was alive.

Taylor made a mental note that she had to go back to Pelican Beach and see the tarot reader as soon as possible. She needed Miriam to know that she'd helped her, and that Angie was going to be okay.

When a doctor came out of the room, Taylor's heart jumped. Maybe this was it. She hurried over to him. The doctor was middle-aged, bald, and wearing a white coat. He looked tired. The lab coat hung off his shoulders, weighted and slumped like himself.

"Is my sister okay?" Taylor asked, her pulse in her throat.

The doctor gave her a lopsided smile, one that didn't signal good news. Taylor's anxiety rose. "She's currently sedated and sleeping," the doctor said. "We've cleaned her up. Unfortunately, your sister's body has endured many traumas. She is severely malnourished, and in dire need of proper nutrition. The physical and psychological trauma she's gone through is difficult for me to explain, but just know she's safe for now. If you'd like, you can go in and see her, but I have to ask you not to touch her or disturb her, or try to wake her up."

Taylor swallowed. This was worse than she could have imagined. No—what would have been worse was if Angie was dead. But she wasn't. Malnourished, yes, but very much alive. Taylor counted her lucky stars.

"I understand," she said.

"I'll be right outside if you need anything," the doctor said.

Taylor nodded, and the doctor left.

Taylor moved to the door. A white curtain hung from a wire, blocking her from whatever was on the other side. She took a deep breath and went into the room, moving the curtain aside and closing the door behind her.

And there, on the white hospital bed, was Angie. Her black hair was no longer matted, but brushed smooth, splayed out around her head on the pillow. And she was breathing softly as she slept. Taylor couldn't believe it.

She slowly made her way toward the bed and pulled up the seat beside Angie.

"I'm sorry," she said, the words barely more than a whisper. "I'm so, so sorry."

She had to find a way to help.

"I know you can hear me. I don't know if this is real, but I don't care. I'm going to talk to you." She slid her hands into her pockets, trying not to let them shake. "I'm your sister, Angie. I'm here for you. I'm sorry for everything you've had to go through, but…I'm here."

Taylor felt herself shutting down, tears welling at the corners of her eyes. "I don't know what to do. I'm so sorry I wasn't here. I'm so sorry. There's so much I want to tell you. And I want you to know that I had a dream about you. And I never stopped looking for you. I want you to know that."

She wiped the tears away, feeling stupid. "I want you to know that…I still need you. We all do. Even Mom and Dad. There's so much to say…"

The words caught in her throat.

Time seemed to slow. Taylor thought of who Angie was before she went missing. How bright and healthy she was. This version of Angie looked so gaunt, so tired. It snapped Taylor's heart in two. What kind of monster could do this? Well, Taylor knew what kind—she'd looked him in the eyes. But she wished he wasn't dead. She wished she could beat the answers out of him, but he was gone. Still, Taylor was haunted by the idea of what he'd been doing to Angie for all these years.

"How could he do this to you? How could he be so horrible?" She closed her eyes, tears burning at the corners. "I'm here for you. I'll help you through this. I'll help you get through this." She opened her eyes and looked at her sister. "I'm always here for you. I'll never leave you."

Angie stirred a little in her sleep, but didn't wake.

"I will help you, Angie. Everything's going to be okay."

Slowly, she reached out and brushed Angie's hair out of her face. Angie didn't stir. "It's going to be okay."

"Taylor?"

Taylor turned around to see her mom and dad in the doorway—and as soon as they saw Angie, their eyes went wide.

"Oh my god," Taylor's mom said. "It's true! Is that—"

"Angie," Taylor's dad said, his voice barely a whisper. "Oh my god, Taylor, you found her."

"I found her," Taylor said, crying.

"She's okay?" Taylor's dad asked.

Taylor nodded. "She's asleep right now, but…she's okay." Her voice was shaky.

"Oh, thank god," Taylor's mom said, and she moved to the bed to hug Angie. "Oh, I've missed you so much. I'm so sorry I wasn't here. But I'm here now. I'm right here."

"She's safe now," Taylor said, her voice cracking.

"No one's ever going to hurt her again," her dad said, and he pulled Taylor into a hug. "Sweetie, you did it. You saved her."

Taylor's eyes welled with tears. This was one of the moments she'd been waiting for. The moment she'd been fighting for. She hadn't just saved Angie for herself—she'd saved her for her parents, who had lost a daughter all those years ago.

And they'd lost a part of themselves with her.

Taylor had always felt so guilty for not being able to find her. She was an FBI agent, after all, but she was never even able to save her own sister.

Until now.

Angie was home. Taylor still couldn't believe it.

Her parents were right there, hugging their daughter. They were so relieved.

"Thank you, sweetheart," Taylor's dad said.

"You have no idea how much this means to us," her mom said. "All this time, we've been wondering if she was alive…if we'd ever see her again. I can't believe my baby girl is alive."

Her parents each covered one side of the hospital bed, each hugging Angie. Taylor leaned against the wall, crying. She wiped away the tears as she watched, feeling as if she were about to fall apart. But she didn't.

She turned away so her parents wouldn't see her weak. But then she felt a hand on her shoulder. She turned to see her dad standing there, a small smile on his face, his eyes red and watery.

"I'm so proud of you," he said. "You've done something amazing. You've saved your sister. We'll take care of her from here. We'll make sure she knows how much we love her."

Angie was going to get help. She was going to get the help she needed to get better.

Taylor smiled. "Thanks, Dad. I know you will."

"I'm pretty sure you're gonna be okay," her dad said. He put his hand on her shoulder. "I want you to go home, okay? You've done enough. You've given your sister the second chance she needed. You've given us the second chance we needed. All of us, as a family. You saved us all, sweetie."

Taylor let out a sob. "I don't wanna go home. I wanna stay here. I wanna be with Angie."

"You need rest too, sweetie," Taylor's mom said, walking over. "We can watch Angie. Don't worry. The doctors said she'll be sleeping for a long time anyway."

"I don't want to leave her," Taylor said.

"You're not leaving her," her mom said. "We're taking care of her now. That's what matters. The fact that you brought her to us. Look what you did. You're amazing, sweetie. If anyone deserves a break, it's you."

Her mom pulled her in for a hug. And Taylor hugged her back. It was true—she needed rest. She'd been running on adrenaline for so long, and she needed to recover.

She'd done what she set out to do. She'd found the sister she'd been searching for.

"I'm very proud of you," her dad said. "You've been through so much, Taylor. Go home and get some rest."

Taylor nodded. "Okay," she said. "I'll go home."

She wiped her eyes and turned away from the bed.

And then she caught a glimpse of herself in the mirror.

Her red eyes, her black hair, and her dirty clothes.

She really did look like a total mess. But she'd won. All her hard work had paid off.

As Taylor left the hospital, she thought of how far she'd come in such a short time. She'd gone from being a girl trying to help her sister, to a girl who found her sister and brought her home. She'd gone from begging her husband to forgive her and stay with her to accepting that it was over. She'd grown as an agent, too, since she moved away from Portland.

It had been a journey, and she was glad she'd gotten to go on it.

But at the same time, Angie still hadn't woken up. Taylor thought of Angie's eyes when she first found her in the cabin—how haunted she'd looked. In truth, Angie had looked at Taylor like she didn't know her at all.

But no—Taylor couldn't afford those negative thoughts.

Angie would wake up soon, and Angie would be okay.

She had to be.

For now, Taylor had one place she needed to go next.

CHAPTER THREE

Taylor pressed her foot on the gas pedal. The sky looked like an oil painting, its orange hues unevenly scattered against the canvas. With the window down, the early autumn air blew into the car, carrying the smell of the beach.

Taylor still hadn't slept. She'd gone back to her parents' for a bit and tried to rest, but her eyes simply wouldn't stay shut. There had been too much going on. But she had some time to kill. And there was one place she knew she needed to visit.

The population sign for Pelican Beach, Virginia, passed by Taylor's car. It was hard to come back here, where she had so many memories with her ex-husband, Ben, whom she was still in the process of divorcing—his idea. But Taylor was more than okay with it all now. She was as over Ben as she'd ever be. They still had to sell their house here, and they hadn't received an offer yet, but Taylor was sure some family would scoop it up and start a beautiful life where Taylor had once wished to have her own.

But Taylor wasn't back in Pelican Beach for Ben or her house or anything like that.

She was here for Miriam Belasco, the tarot reader who had helped her so many times.

If it weren't for Miriam, Taylor wouldn't have found Angie. It was Miriam who'd drawn the symbol that led Taylor to the cabin. Taylor owed her her life.

Taylor's car passed through the small downtown core of Pelican Beach. The sunrise in the distance created a haze over the ocean, where the waves hammered the shore and grew louder. The town looked the same—and different at the same time. Taylor remembered this place when it was a tourist attraction and a community. The town had a musical vibe, with jazz music and blues spilling out of the bars.

She had so many memories of her time in this place—her time with Ben—and she clung to those, even as she tried to stretch into a better future. Taylor pulled into the parking lot up the street from Belasco's shop, then got out of her car into the cool morning.

It was October now and the leaves would soon die. Taylor had moved here in the summer. It felt like another life had passed her since she walked down that boardwalk with Ben, since she visited Belasco for the first time.

But everything had happened. And now she was here again, on a different path than she had planned.

Taylor approached the door of the shop. On the last case she was working, with the missing girls on Brock Island, Taylor had gone in with Miriam Belasco's warnings, but had ended up doing her own tarot reading on the island that, in some way, had helped her out on the case. But Taylor was clearly not a skilled reader, and maybe she'd just been looking for things that weren't there.

Taylor believed in Belasco, though. They'd been through enough together at this point for Taylor to know that everything Belasco said, in some way, had truth to it.

Taylor took a deep breath and entered the shop. The familiar smell of incense swallowed her, and the same purple and gold curtains separated the front desk from the back room.

Belasco emerged through the curtains. It still amazed Taylor that someone so young could be so wise. She looked at Taylor through her long, dark lashes.

"Ms. Sage… you're back," she said.

"I wanted to talk to you about something," Taylor said, not quite sure how to explain what had happened. "There's been an update. A major one."

"Come back to the table." Belasco's black hair bounced with each step. "I'm glad you came. I've been waiting for you."

The back room smelled of incense and flowers. Taylor recognized the smell of tiger lilies from the last time she'd been here, when she'd seen the cards that had foretold of her journey to Brock Island.

Taylor sat down. She didn't know how to come out with what she'd found. "How have you been?"

"Doing well, thanks. I just made a fresh pot of tea. Would you like some?"

"Sure, thank you."

Belasco brought the tea over, then sat down across from Taylor. The light from a burning candle hit her face, making her look even younger. "So, what is this update?" Belasco had catlike eyes that seemed to look right into Taylor's soul. Part of Taylor wondered if

Belasco somehow already knew the truth. It wouldn't surprise her. She really was a mysterious woman.

Taylor took a deep breath and said it anyway: "My sister—Angie. I found her. She's alive."

Belasco smiled. It sent a rush of relief through Taylor. "I'm so glad. It's what I saw. It's what I sensed. I'm so glad you found her."

"I don't know how it's possible that she's still alive," Taylor said. "But she is. She's in the hospital recovering, but she's alive, Miriam. And I don't think I would have found her without your help."

"I told you that what you were feeling was real. And I'm glad you were able to find her. You're very intuitive. And, you know, people come back to us from the other side. You've seen it happen."

Taylor smiled. Her chest was warm. She still couldn't believe it. "I don't know how to thank you," Taylor said. "Can I pay you? Is there anything I can do?"

"I'm just happy for you. I'm glad you can be reunited with your sister. No payment is necessary." Belasco looked down at the many different necklaces she wore. She lifted a charm of a purple and gold butterfly. "The butterfly is a symbol of transformation," Belasco said. "It's a sign of continuing life through death. Your sister is still alive—but something has changed."

"You mean, because she's alive?"

"Because she's become something else—a butterfly. She's in a different state of being. But she's still with us, and she seems to be guiding you. The cards were right, Taylor. You were meant to find your sister."

Taylor's eyes watered a little. It was strange to have her sister back—and to have her be a butterfly. But somehow, it felt right. She just hoped Angie would wake up soon so Taylor could truly talk to her.

"But please, I have to pay you somehow," Taylor said. "Or maybe we can do another reading now, and I can pay you for that?"

Belasco smiled. "I'd be happy to do another reading for you." The tarot cards were positioned in front of her, and she picked them up and shuffled them. Taylor watched eagerly. So many things in her life had been solved. For one, Angie was back. Two, her divorce was being finalized. And three, she wasn't currently working a case. So whatever the cards had to say would be interesting; it might point to something more personal to Taylor's life. She was eager to see.

"The first card is the ace of wands," Belasco said. "The ace represents your energy, your drive, your ambition. There may be a time when you have to make a choice, have to make a move, have to be the first one to try something. It will be difficult, and you'll be nervous, but you need to do it."

"Okay," Taylor said. She was a little nervous—but more to the point, she was eager to know what was next.

Belasco picked up the next card. "The Tower. This represents a period of change, unexpected problems and unfortunate situations that may knock you down, but you need to get back up. Take this time to decide what you really want. The old way of doing things is no longer working for you. You're going to have to do something new."

Taylor nodded. She was going through a lot of "new" things…

And finally, Belasco flipped up the last card. A grim expression took over her face.

"Is it bad?" Taylor asked, her heart in her throat.

"It's the three of swords." Belasco closed her eyes and shook her head. "There's a betrayal coming." Her voice was grim. "If I were you, I would watch my back for the next little while. Don't let anyone know where you are. And—I'm sorry to have to say this—but I think someone you love might be working against you."

Taylor's face fell. "But… who?"

"That's the thing. I don't know. I can't see. It might not even be someone you know. Or maybe you will find out more soon. I don't know everything." Belasco reached out and squeezed Taylor's hand. Her cat eyes looked even more sad. "I know this is a lot. You've just received good news about your sister, so don't let the reading discourage you. I'm not really sure what they all mean."

"You're not sure?" Taylor asked, trying to wrap her mind around it.

"Tarot readings don't always make sense," Belasco said. "They're open to interpretation. A lot of it is just feeling. You know this." She shrugged. "I'm sorry. I wish I could give you more."

"No, it's okay," Taylor said. She was trying to convince herself as much as she was trying to convince Belasco. "But thanks for looking out for me. I'll take it all into account."

Even with the warning, she felt a little better. She was glad to at least know what she was dealing with. Angie was alive. Taylor just had to keep her sister safe, whatever that meant.

***

The drive home felt like it was taking forever. Taylor couldn't get the reading out of her mind. She kept replaying it, trying to piece it together, trying to figure out who could be working against her. But she had no answers.

Suddenly, a phone call came in. Taylor's phone was connected to the Bluetooth on her car, and the screen displayed Wesley's number. Damn. She'd been hoping it was the hospital.

But Taylor had completely forgotten that last night, as she'd gone into the cabin, she'd sent her partner, Special Agent John Wesley, an SOS text which he'd never responded to. Taylor was up all through the night, and it was now only nine a.m., so maybe Wesley hadn't checked his phone until now.

Taylor pressed accept. "This is Taylor Sage."

"Sage," Wesley said. "I just got your text. I'm sorry, I—"

"Wes, it's okay," Taylor cut in. She smiled, thinking about what happened. "I'll explain everything when I see you."

"Jesus, Taylor," he said. "Winchester said you found your sister."

"It's true, Wes. I did."

"Damn… I don't know what to say. You need to fill me in on what happened. You heading to Quantico today?"

"I don't know. I need to check on my sister. She's in the hospital."

"Okay. Well, if you're coming into work, Winchester said we have a case. I think he mentioned he was going to let you off the hook, but you would obviously be welcome if you want to work."

Taylor paused. The last thing she was thinking about right now was work—for once. "He did?"

Wesley sighed. "Look, I… I can't imagine what you're going through. If you need more time, I can probably work this thing alone. There's no pressure from me. I've got your back."

Taylor bit her lip as she drove. She didn't want to leave Wesley hanging. But at the same time, there was too much happening in her life.

"Let me call you back," she said.

"Roger that."

They hung up. The first thing Taylor did was use her voice activation to call the hospital.

"Yes, I'm calling to check on the status of Angela Sage? She was admitted yesterday. This is her sister, Taylor."

The nurse on the other end sounded like she was chewing gum. Taylor tried to be patient.

"I'm sorry, Ms. Sage, but Angela is currently resting. It says here on her file that she has not woken up, but her parents—your parents—are with her."

"I'm coming to see her," Taylor said.

"Well, the file says it's best if Angela is just with her parents when she wakes."

"What? Why?" Taylor's blood burned. They couldn't just keep her away from Angie. Not after everything she'd gone through.

"Hold on, Ms. Sage," the nurse said. "Let me get the doctor."

A moment later, a different voice, a man's, came on the line. This must be the doctor from earlier. "Ms. Sage? This is Doctor Abrams."

"What's going on with Angie?"

"Your sister is doing well, all things considered," the doctor said. "But we would like to keep her calm when she wakes up."

"Calm?" Taylor asked. "What do you mean?"

"Angie was involved in a very traumatic event," the doctor said. "We don't want to overwhelm her when she wakes up."

"So you're saying I can't see her?" Taylor asked, her frustration mounting. Taylor hadn't gone through all of this to be held back from her sister. It was too cruel.

"It would be best if you stayed away for now," the doctor said. "Your parents are with her, and she's getting the best care possible. You will absolutely be able to see her soon, but Angie still hasn't woken up, and even when she does, we're unlikely to discharge her for at least a few more days."

Taylor paused. The doctor did have a point. "I understand," Taylor said.

"That's good." The doctor's voice was kind. "I'm sure we'll talk again soon."

With that, Dr. Abrams hung up. Taylor was left anxious in highway traffic. She was so close to her sister, but she couldn't see her. Frustration coursed through her. But Taylor was powerless to do anything else. She needed to do what was best for Angie, and if that meant staying away, then so be it.

But Taylor would drive herself mad waiting around for updates. She needed to keep herself occupied.

And there was no better way to do that than to get back to work.

CHAPTER FOUR

Taylor walked into the Quantico base with her head high, ready to hear about whatever case was on the table. She briskly walked into the briefing room, where Wesley was waiting for her. He stood tall when she entered. Taylor was always still amazed at how large, yet warm Wesley was. He hadn't seemed warm at all when she'd first met him, but she had to admit, he'd grown on her.

"Sage, you're here," he said.

Taylor smiled. "Hi, Wes. I'm here."

Wesley had helped Taylor immensely on the last case in Brock Island, and she wouldn't forget that anytime soon. When she saw him, tall, tanned, and dark-haired, she felt a strange sense of familiarity inside of her. Wesley's steely gray eyes locked on hers. Taylor shook the feeling away.

"Your sister," Wesley said, rubbing the back of his neck. "She's really alive, Sage. Damn… you must be over the moon."

Taylor smiled. "Yeah. I found her. Over the moon isn't even half of it… part of me still feels like I'm dreaming."

"But how? What happened?" He walked closer to her until Taylor had to look up at him. "And why didn't you ask for my help sooner? Or call me? I would've been there, but my phone was on silent, and I just didn't see the text."

There was so much about everything in Taylor's life that she couldn't just explain to Wesley. The tarot readings. The signs. How she'd figured out where Angie was. He'd either never believe her or think she was crazy, but either way, Taylor gave him a smile. "It was a lot of things, honestly, but I was going through our old family photos and I saw something familiar. I decided to check it out on a hunch, but then… Angie was really there."

"Seriously? A hunch was all it took?" Wesley's thick eyebrows rose.

He was clearly not buying it. He'd be right not to. It was so much more than that, but how could Taylor even begin explaining?

"There has to be more than that," Wesley said. "Why didn't you call me? I thought after all the stuff on Brock Island, you'd at least trust me enough to do that."

Confusion cluttered Taylor's mind. Wesley didn't seem mad, but he did seem put off, his face twisted as he looked away. A strange, warm feeling flooded Taylor's heart.

He cares...

"Anyway," Wesley muttered when Taylor didn't answer, "they get an ID on the kidnapper yet?"

"Not yet," Taylor said. "He shot himself in the head on the scene. I'm still waiting for details. Local police over there are in charge, as it's their jurisdiction. The FBI is involved too, but obviously, it's not in my hands."

"Damn. That's brutal."

It was. Taylor had barely spent any time thinking about the horrific events in the cabin because she'd been so ecstatic just to know Angie was actually alive. But there was still more work to be done, more answers to be discovered.

For now, Taylor had no choice but to step back and let the other officers and the FBI do their work. Taylor was too close to the case to be on it officially, for obvious reasons.

But she did have one question for Wesley:

"So what's this about a new case?"

"Your guess is as good as mine," Wesley said. "I'm still waiting on—"

Chief Steven Winchester burst into the room, as if on cue. Taylor and Wesley both stood at attention. Winchester's handlebar mustache had grown longer since Taylor had last seen him, and he was wearing a tweed suit. Short blond hair shone in the light of the room.

"Special Agent Wesley," he said, then his eyes fell on Taylor, and he broke into a smile. Taylor was stunned as Winchester came over and trapped her in a bear hug. "You're gonna have to forgive me for being so unprofessional, but congratulations are in order, Special Agent Sage."

Taylor's face heated. She was definitely not a hugger. Winchester broke away and gave her a slap on the shoulder with a hearty laugh. "Your sister's alive, damn it. That's fantastic news."

"Thanks, Chief," Taylor said. "It's been a wild ride, to say the least."

"Right, well." Winchester glanced at both agents. "I'd love to have a drink to celebrate, but unfortunately, it's business as usual over here. As you two have been informed, we have a new case."

Taylor's chest twisted. She hoped it wouldn't be a bad one, but in her line of work, she was always prepared to deal with the macabre.

"A small city around thirty minutes from here in Virginia," Winchester said. "Called Flyway City. Actually, they have one of the lowest crime rates in the country… so when two women were randomly killed in alleyways, it turned heads."

Taylor exchanged a look with Wesley. This did not sound good.

"But it appears to be done by the same guy," Winchester said. "Both happened in an alleyway, and it looks like the women were somehow snuck up on. No sign of a struggle."

"Cause of death?" Taylor asked, unsure if she really wanted the answer. Right now, she didn't want to think about murder—she wanted to rush to the hospital and see Angie. But she knew she couldn't do that, and if there was a killer on the loose, then someone had to stop him before he killed again.

"A single slit to the throat," Winchester said. "Not pretty."

Damn. It was one thing to kill someone by shooting them or even by stabbing them in the chest, but to slit their throat… it was like the person had no remorse at all.

Taylor couldn't even begin to express how she felt.

Her first case after coming back from Brock Island, and it was a serial killer? No wonder Wes had looked so conflicted when he'd seen her. Even if he hadn't known the specifics of the case, he knew there was a chance it would be a bad one.

She hated that she had to deal with this now. At the same time, this was her calling. It was basically in her DNA. Taylor was kidding herself if she thought she could stay off work for even a little while.

"The thing is," Winchester said, his voice grim, "the killer is getting away with it. He's never left a single shred of evidence behind. No fingerprints, no DNA on the scene, no witnesses, nothing, at least not yet. We've got forensics at the crime scene now." Winchester's eyes hardened. "And that's where you two come in. I need you to get down to the crime scene and see what you make of all this."

Taylor swallowed. "We'll head down right away."

"Good," Winchester said. "I know it's not exactly a vacation, but it could be good for you two to get back in the field. There will be plenty of time to rest… after you catch this guy."

"Will do, Chief," Taylor said. She needed the distraction anyway, and she was glad to know that the case wasn't too far away—Angie would still be within Taylor's reach if she got the call from the hospital.

For now, she had a killer to catch.

***

Taylor adjusted herself in the passenger seat of Wesley's car. He'd insisted on driving, although he'd been quiet since they left HQ. The mid-morning sky was awash with blue streaks, and the highway was surprisingly empty. The bright, bold blue of the sky was like a protective dome, shielding the earth below.

Taylor glanced at Wesley as he drove. His black hair had grown out a bit recently. Taylor remembered when she met him, it had been short, military style, but it looked like he was due for a trim.

She couldn't help but think about earlier, when he'd seemed put off by her not asking him more adamantly for help. Did he actually care that much?

"Hey, Wes," Taylor said.

He shot her a glance, then refocused on the road. "Yeah?"

"Sorry I didn't call you," she said. "The text wasn't enough. I know you would've backed me up. We're partners, and you were there with me all the way in Brock Island."

His expression tightened for a moment, and he looked back to the road. "I know, I just… I don't exactly deal well with things like that."

"That's because you're an FBI agent." Taylor gave him a teasing smile. "So you're doing a great job of being one now."

Wesley laughed, but it was empty. "I guess so."

"Hey, listen, I—" Taylor stopped.

He turned toward her, his brow furrowed. "Sage?"

"I'm sorry if I seemed like I didn't trust you," Taylor said. "I care about you, and I trust you wholeheartedly."

"But you don't trust me enough to tell me the truth," Wesley said. "I know you found your sister on more than a hunch, Taylor. You don't solve a two-decade-old missing persons case on a hunch."

Taylor was startled by his words, her stomach twisting at the truth. "I know this may seem crazy… but I can't tell you all of it. It's just too personal."

"It doesn't," Wesley said. "You're an intelligent woman, Sage, and the truth is, sometimes I wish you'd let me in. I know there's more to the story about how you found your sister. You don't trust me enough to tell me."

Was it about trust? Taylor wasn't sure. She ran her hand through her black hair, adjusting her bangs. They needed a trim.

In a way, Taylor supposed she didn't trust Wesley because she didn't trust him to believe her if she told him what had really happened. It was a lot to ask. Taylor had been cynical once, and anything extraordinary she would immediately pass off as coincidence or plain fake. But Miriam Belasco had changed all that. And now Taylor had the tarot cards to thank for Angie being home.

There was no easy way to explain that.

"Anyway, sorry," Wesley said. "I'm being out of line."

"You're not. I appreciate you caring. Really." Taylor shot him a smile. "Give me some time."

Wesley nodded. "I can do that."

Taylor focused on the road passing by outside the car; the fields of green beyond the highway, topped by the blue morning sky. She checked her phone. No calls from the hospital or texts from her parents. She could only assume Angie was still sleeping.

Miriam's reading entered her mind; her warning about a "betrayal." Taylor wondered what it could be, and she couldn't stop herself from worrying if it was a warning not to trust the hospital with Angie. But that was ridiculous, right? She'd met the doctors, and they seemed like honest people. It had to be about something else.

She sighed. At least now she had a case to focus on—but she hoped, for the sake of the women in Flyway City, that she would catch this bastard sooner rather than later.

Maybe it was a bad idea for Taylor to take on a case with everything going on, but she had to do this.

She wouldn't let them down.

CHAPTER FIVE

Wesley had never seen such a creepy sign in his life. A clown face looked down at him from above the toy store's entrance and sent a shiver up his spine.

He felt bad for the poor woman who'd lost her life here, of all places. This was not a pretty spot to end it all, that was for sure.

A ribbon of caution tape barred off the alleyway and a throng of cops milled about. Wesley lifted the caution tape, allowing Taylor to pass under, then slipped under it himself. He and Taylor held up their badges as they approached a tall officer with a thin mustache.

The officer's eyes narrowed as he took in their badges. "I didn't realize the feds were already here."

"We're here to see the body," Taylor said, straight to the point.

The officer's mustache twitched. "You'll have to talk to Detective Reynolds. He's in charge of the case."

He gestured down the alleyway, where a heavyset man in a rumpled suit was talking to a couple of uniformed officers.

"Thanks," Wesley muttered.

He and Taylor made their way down the alleyway. The scent of garbage, urine, and sewage filled the alley like a miasma. The odors were sharp in the cool air.

"Detective Reynolds?" Taylor called out.

The man turned, and Wesley saw that he had a wart on the end of his nose. Looked like a standard detective-type, though, and Wesley doubted he'd be thrilled to hand his case over to the FBI.

"That's me," the detective said. "You must be the feds."

He held out his hand and they shook.

"I'm Special Agent Taylor Sage, and this is my partner, Special Agent Wesley," Taylor said.

"Pleased to meet you," Detective Reynolds said. "What can I do for you?"

"We'd like to see the body," Taylor said.

The detective's brow furrowed. "Well, okay, but…"

"But what?" Wesley asked.

"It's… pretty gruesome," the detective said. Reynolds was a giant of a man, with a broad, meaty face and a belly that strained the buttons on his suit. He scratched the back of his neck and looked uncomfortable. "The woman was brutally murdered. I mean, the wound was clean, but it's just a sad sight to see."

"We've seen our share of gruesome things," Taylor said.

The detective hesitated, then shrugged. "All right, if you insist. Come this way."

They followed him a short way up the alley. Wesley was unnerved, that was for sure. He hated seeing dead women. At the same time, sometimes they reminded him of everything he was fighting to protect. Maisie, his daughter… Wesley would do anything for her.

They drew closer to the body. It was a young woman lying on her back with her eyes wide open. There was a deep gash across her throat, and Wesley could see the glint of bone. He swallowed hard, fighting the urge to vomit.

"Jesus," Taylor muttered.

"Told you it wasn't pretty," Reynolds muttered.

Wesley faced him. "Can you tell us what happened?"

Reynolds's gaze shifted from Taylor to Wesley. "A man called nine one one early this morning to report a woman down in the alley," he said. "On arriving, we found the woman lying here dead, her throat slit, the poor thing."

"Do we have an ID?" Wesley asked.

"Yeah." Reynolds sighed. "Mary Gibbons. Twenty-six. She owned a flower shop just up the road, and her car was parked nearby. We think she was leaving work when the killer lured her into this alleyway."

"How long has she been dead?" Taylor asked.

"We won't know until the coroner arrives, but I'd say she died somewhere in the night." Reynolds took a deep breath. "Whoever killed her did a real number on her."

"Do we have any suspects?" Taylor asked.

Reynolds shook his head. "Not yet. They didn't find the guy's prints, so for now we don't have anything. We're canvassing the neighborhood, but no leads yet."

Wesley studied the body. Damn… that poor girl. "Any idea what kind of weapon the killer used?"

"Not yet," the detective said. "But judging from the wound, it was a pretty sharp knife."

The alleyway was too dark for Wesley's liking, and he couldn't stand the smell of piss and garbage. He felt a chill, despite the warmth of the morning sun.

"He probably attacked her from behind," Taylor said. She kneeled in front of the body, getting a closer look. Wesley stood back and let her work. "Her hair… it's so neat at the front, but the back…" Taylor shifted the girl's head slightly. "It's all bunched up. I think he grabbed her by the hair and jerked her head back, exposing her throat. Probably slit her throat from left to right, then let her go."

Taylor stood up, her face grim. Wesley nodded. That seemed like the right situation. But one thing was unclear to him:

"How'd he even get her here?" he asked. "There's not a lot of traffic on this road, and the alley's a dead end. No one would have just let a killer lead them off into a dark alley."

Reynolds shrugged. "Maybe she knew him?"

Wesley glanced at Taylor. She did not look convinced.

"I don't know," Taylor said. "I have a feeling she was lured here. But maybe he did just drag her…" She turned and looked at the detective. "Have you checked the surrounding area? Maybe there's something there."

"Yeah, we've searched, but we didn't find anything." Reynolds sighed. "This is a pretty quiet road. If we don't find something on the street, we'll have to widen our search."

"If we're going to search the neighborhood, can you arrange for some extra manpower?" Taylor said.

Reynolds nodded. "I'll get on it."

"Detective, before you go," Taylor said. "This isn't the first victim, right?"

"Right," the detective said. "There was another girl. Same circumstances, different alley. All the files have been uploaded and should be in the database."

"Thanks," Wesley said.

Detective Reynolds nodded and hurried off to his car. Taylor turned to Wesley. "Come on, let's go back to the car. We have to get to work."

As they walked back to the car, Wesley couldn't help but feel uneasy. "Do you think this is the work of a serial killer?" he asked, even though it seemed obvious that was the case. Two similar kills in such a short span of time was ugly.

"I don't know," Taylor said. "But we need to find out who did this, and fast, before another girl dies."

Wesley nodded in agreement as they got to the street and reached the car. The sun shone off the windshield and into Wesley's eyes as he got in, Taylor on the passenger side. She immediately took out her laptop, and Wesley was impressed she was able to keep her head in the game, considering all that was going on in her personal life.

It was incredible—damn near impossible—that Taylor had been able to locate her sister, and the inner detective in Wesley wanted to know how she did it more than anything. He knew there were things Taylor wasn't telling him still. She was such a mysterious person, and he couldn't help but be drawn to her. The fact that she was such a beautiful woman didn't help.

Wesley opened his laptop, knowing Taylor was doing the same. He caught her looking at him out of the corner of his eye and found himself staring back, but Taylor looked away. Her eyes were a deep gray-blue, the color of the ocean in the morning, and was probably the most eye-catching thing about her. Her skin was milky white, with a hint of freckles across her nose and cheeks. This, combined with her black hair, made her stunning.

Wes turned away before Taylor could catch him staring. What was he thinking? He needed to get it together.

"So what now?" Wesley asked, as Taylor started her computer. "What are we going to do?"

Taylor turned to him. "Well, I definitely want to know more about the first victim, but let's focus on the most recent first." She scanned the file. "We need to talk to the guy who found her this morning. Maybe he saw something."

"You think he'll talk?"

"If he's not too traumatized, yeah. If he saw something, we need to know."

"You got an address?" Wesley asked.

"Yeah, right here. Says he's a garbage man, found her while on the job. I have his address here. I doubt he just went back to work after that, so let's try his house."

"Good enough for me," Wesley said.

He started the car, and they headed off. The neighborhood was quiet and friendly, with the occasional house cat lazing about in the sun. Wesley saw a kid playing with a soccer ball, a lovely older woman sitting on her porch, and a man biking down the street. It was a beautiful neighborhood, really, and the last thing he expected was that a brutal murder would have happened here.

Wesley thought of his daughter, Maisie, back home with his ex. He thought of how devastated he'd be if anything bad ever happened to either of them. He and his ex weren't best friends or anything, but as the mother of his child, she was still family. Wesley would do anything to protect his daughter and her mother.

"Hey," Taylor said, grabbing his attention. "You hear me?"

"Huh?" Wesley said, having no idea what the question was.

"I said, we're here." Taylor pointed to a house across the road.

Wesley sighed. "All right. Let's do this."

The garbage truck was parked in front of a tidy little house. It was small, with a modest front yard and a driveway full of cars. Wesley parked the car across the street and killed the engine.

They got out of the car, and Taylor led Wesley up the drive. The house's front door was wide open, and they could hear music playing from within. A man stood on the front porch, drinking a can of soda. He turned to face them. He was grizzled and in his forties, wearing his garbage truck uniform still. Clearly, after discovering the crime, he hadn't returned to work, but also hadn't fully recovered.

"Morning," Wesley said as they walked up.

The garbage man was shaken up, but nodded at them. "I take it you're here to talk about…"

Taylor and Wesley both held up their badges.

"We're with the FBI," Taylor said. "Can you tell us what you found this morning?"

"I… I don't know if I can."

"It's all right," Taylor said gently. "Just take your time."

The garbage man, a gruff but kind-hearted man, nodded and led them inside. He sat down at his kitchen table, and they sat across from him. The table was cluttered with dirty dishes and empty beer bottles. A stack of bills was piled high next to the sink.

"I was just doing my usual route," he began slowly. "Collecting the trash cans and taking them to the truck. When I got to the alley, I saw her. She was lying there, in a pool of blood." He took a deep breath and continued on. "I didn't get too close, but I could tell she was dead. Her throat had been slit."

The garbage man looked away, clearly still upset by what he had seen.

"Did you see anyone else around?" Wesley asked.

The garbage man shook his head. "No, no one. It was just her lying there in the alley. I didn't see anything. I didn't hear anything either. I just found her there, dead."

Wesley and Taylor exchanged a look. This wasn't anything new, unfortunately.

"Is there anything else you can think of that might be helpful?" Wesley asked.

The garbage man shook his head. "No, that's everything… I swear, if I saw more, I'd let ya know. I feel so bad for Mary. I've bought flowers from her shop before."

Wesley nodded. "It's a shame what happened to her, but we'll do our best to make sure it doesn't happen again."

"I hope you do, Agents," he said. "The women in this town don't deserve this."

Wesley and Taylor thanked him for his time and went back outside to their car parked on the road. The sky was open and clear, but a chill ran through the early October air. Wesley went to the driver's side, Taylor the passenger side, but neither of them got into the car. Taylor had a pinched expression, and Wesley knew what that meant.

"What are you thinking, Sage?" He rested his arms on top of the car.

"I'm thinking that these attacks feel random," she said. "More like crimes of opportunity than anything. These women seem to have no connection, and anyone could have passed by these public places. Sometimes those attacks can be even more dangerous than the preplanned because it means no one is safe." Taylor met Wesley's eyes. "We better get this guy, and we better do it fast. Let's go talk to the family of the victim."

They got in the car, and Wesley strapped in. Visiting families was never easy—but it had to be done.

It was like the garbage man had said; the women in this town didn't deserve to live in fear. And they definitely didn't deserve to be killed by some psycho.

Wesley would put a stop to this. He swore it on his life.

CHAPTER SIX

Taylor's heart stalled as Wesley pulled into the driveway of the Gibbons' home. Mary, though twenty-six, lived at home with her parents still. The house was small and quaint, with blue walls and more flowers in the garden than Taylor had ever seen.

Mary had seemed like a sweet young woman who just wanted to work in her flower shop. She didn't deserve her brutal ending. Taylor's fists clenched as Wesley put the car in park. No one deserved murder, but it hurt especially when it happened to someone who seemed to do nothing but bring joy to the world. Taylor wished she could turn back the clock and change things. But she couldn't; she could only try to take this guy down and ensure no one else met the same fate as Mary.

They walked up to the door and knocked gently, the sound echoing in the still morning air. The door was opened by an older woman with kind eyes that were full of tears. She was wearing a flowered dress and a white apron. Her hair was pulled back in a tight bun.

"Yes, can I help you?" she asked.

"We're here about Mary," Taylor said, holding up her badge. "We're so sorry for your loss."

The woman's face crumpled, and she began to cry. "Oh, my baby girl. Come in, please."

She led them into the house and had them sit down in the living room. The room was cozy and comfortable, with a well-loved couch and a soft rug. A fire crackled in the fireplace, and the warm light danced in the shadows. There were pictures of Mary everywhere, and her mother kept touching them as she talked, pacing around the room.

"She was such a good girl," she said through her tears. "Never gave us a day of trouble. It's just not fair."

"Do you have any idea who might've wanted to hurt her?" Taylor asked gently.

Mrs. Gibbons shook her head and wiped her eyes with a tissue as she fell onto the sofa. "No, no one that I can think of. You don't understand… Mary was loved by everyone. And I mean everyone. Even the meanest people you can think of would have smiled at Mary if she gave them a flower. She was pure."

A man walked into the room then, and Taylor could see the resemblance between him and Mary. He had the same blue eyes and kind face.

"What's going on?" he asked, looking from his wife to the two strangers.

"They are with the FBI," she said, her voice shaking. "They're here about Mary."

He sank down onto the couch next to her and put his head in his hands. "Oh, God," he whispered. "Our poor Mary…"

Taylor's heart ached for this family that was grieving so deeply. They had lost their daughter in the most violent way possible, and she vowed to do everything in her power to find out who did this to Mary and make them pay.

Taylor leaned forward. "I know this is hard for you, but we need to ask you these questions. It might seem like a lot, but Mary is counting on us to find the man who killed her."

The parents nodded, their posture stiff.

"Did Mary have a boyfriend?" Wesley asked.

Mrs. Gibbons shook her head. "No. Truth be told, Mary had no interest in romance or dating. She just wanted to work at her store. It was her dream. We helped her raise the money to open it up."

Mr. Gibbons sniffled, balling his fists. "She finally had everything she wanted…"

Taylor's throat tightened. This was all too cruel. She wished none of them had to go through it. Mary sounded like a nice person—and Taylor knew how nice, attractive young women could catch the eye of evil men.

"Was there anyone who was maybe obsessed with Mary?" Taylor asked. "She was a beautiful young woman. Maybe there were men she had rejected?"

"It's possible," Mrs. Gibbons said, "but I do think she would've told us if anyone had given her a hard time. Mary never told us anything about anyone strange. Only that she loved working."

Taylor nodded, thinking on it. More and more, this was looking like a crime of opportunity. Mary could've just been in the wrong place at the wrong time. The killer, whoever he was, chose her because he was there… not because he'd selected her. Taylor wasn't sure which scenario was worse.

"Did Mary ever mention anything about being followed or anyone watching her?" Wesley asked.

The parents shook their heads again.

"No," Mr. Gibbons said, his voice breaking. "Never."

Taylor sighed and sat back in her chair. There didn't seem to be any more answers here.

"Thank you for your time," she said softly. "And again, I'm so sorry for your loss."

Mrs. Gibbons nodded, but she was already lost in her thoughts, staring off into the distance. Taylor and Wesley got up to leave, feeling the weight of this family's grief with them.

Before they left, Taylor turned back to the Gibbons. "We'll find who did this," she promised them. "I swear it."

The Gibbons nodded. "Thank you," they both said.

On their way out, Wesley put a hand on Taylor's shoulder. "You're doing really good," he told her. "It can't be easy to work a case like this with everything going on."

His hand was warm on her shoulder. Taylor wasn't used to being close to people physically, but she appreciated the gesture. It was true; in some ways, the Gibbons reminded Taylor of her own parents, and how devastated they'd been when Angie was taken all those years ago. But in many ways, the Gibbons had it worse, because they knew without a doubt that their daughter was gone.

"Thanks, Wes," Taylor muttered.

Once outside, they walked up to the car, and Taylor's mind raced over what to do next. Both of these crimes had happened close to each other—and both bodies would still be in the coroner's office. Taylor paused. Maybe if there were no clues at the crime scenes themselves, there would be something on the actual victims.

It was morbid, but Taylor had an idea of where do go next.

"Wesley," she said, turning to him. "I think we should go to the coroner's office."

***

Taylor led Wesley into the coroner's office, and they went to the front desk, where a plump woman with wiry black hair sat, reading a magazine. The room smelled like formaldehyde and death, making Taylor's stomach roll.

"Can I help you?" the secretary asked, not looking up from her reading.

Taylor cleared her throat. "We're with the FBI," she said, flashing her badge. "We're here to see the bodies from the recent murders."

The woman had a grim expression, but she nodded and got up from her seat, walking over to a locked door. She opened it with a key and then motioned for them to follow her. "Right this way," she said. "Keep going up the hall, first door on the right. The coroner should be in there now."

With that, the woman left, letting the door slam behind her.

Taylor shuddered involuntarily when she realized that they were in the morgue alone. She knew she was an agent and had seen a lot of bodies, but that never necessarily made it easier. She could still remember the first time she saw a dead body. The young girl had been found shot dead in the street. It had been one of the worst murders Taylor had ever seen, and it had stuck with her for a long time.

Taylor and her former partner in Portland, Jenkins, had spent hours at the scene, trying to find every shred of evidence they could to catch the murderer. The coroner had tried to get them to leave, but Taylor wouldn't have it. Only after they had gone over every inch of that little girl's body had they been able to leave and get some answers.

Eventually, they had found the five men responsible, but it had cost them a large part of the case. The gang members had been smart, and had used false addresses and driver's licenses. It had taken them weeks to find a pattern, and eventually they had found the men living in a house together.

The girl had been a mistake, and they were furious when they were caught. But they were all put in jail for life. Justice had been served. But Taylor had never been able to forget the face of that girl.

Shaking herself from the memory, she focused on the current task. Wesley walked ahead of her, taking long strides. Taylor hurried to catch up. When they reached the door the coroner had told them to go to, they knocked. A deep, gravelly voice told them to come in. Taylor entered first, trying to get her bearings.

The coroner was a tall man with a thick beard, and he was wearing scrubs. He was also wearing a surgical mask and gloves, which looked odd. Taylor tried not to stare.

"Can I help you?" the coroner asked, looking up from his desk. He was sitting in front of a computer.

There was a man on a gurney in the center of the room. He looked to be in his forties, and he was covered in dark marks. This man's death had been violent—the coroner was clearly performing an autopsy when he stepped away to do some paperwork. Taylor swallowed.

"We're with the FBI," Taylor said, flashing her badge. "We need your help with a case. The two young women who were murdered in the alleyways."

"Oh, yes." The coroner's face was grim. "I have them in the other room. Please follow me."

His footsteps were heavy, echoing through the long corridors. Wesley and Taylor followed behind him, not talking. This was not a happy place.

They wound their way through the halls for a few minutes, passing a few open doors. Taylor could see that the rooms were filled cold lockers. Some of them were open and others were shut. The coroner stopped at a door and then unlocked it, pushing it open. Inside were more cold lockers, and the room was freezing.

"This is where we keep the bodies," the coroner said, his voice echoing in the room. "They're all in here."

He led them over to one of the open lockers and pulled out a sheet, revealing the body of a young woman—the same young woman Taylor saw in the alleyway earlier. Except now, her blood had been cleaned away.

"This is Mary Gibbons," he said, pointing to the now clean gash on her neck.

Taylor felt her stomach churn. This was getting to be too much. She turned away, trying not to think about the fact that this had once been a person—someone with a life and a family who loved them. It was strange to see Mary again, all cleaned up. Earlier, there had still been some color on her face, but now she was cold, lifeless.

"And this is the other victim, Emily Johnson," the coroner said, pulling out another sheet. "Same situation with the alleyway killer."

Emily looked so young. She couldn't have been more than twenty-five. Taylor's heart ached for these women and their families.

"This one, we've already performed an autopsy on," the coroner explained. "There were no drugs or alcohol in her system."

"So they were both sober when they were killed?" Wesley asked.

The coroner nodded. "As far as we can tell, yes."

"What about their injuries?" Taylor inquired. "Were they the same?"

"Identical," said the coroner. "A single slit to the throat. Very clean. It looks like the women were snuck up on."

Taylor thought back to the crime scene earlier. It was obvious that Mary had been killed where she was standing, as there was no evidence of a struggle and the blood pattern clearly showed that the body was not moved.

"So how did he get them in the alleyway?" Taylor wondered aloud.

"No idea," the coroner said. "But based on the wound pattern, it does look like they were snuck up on and killed in one fell swoop, so to speak." He pursed his lips and looked down at the bodies. "Real grisly stuff."

Taylor couldn't agree more. As much as it pained her, she leaned in to get a closer look at the gash across the victims' throats. Earlier, she'd thought that the back of Mary's hair had looked messed up, like the killer had grabbed her from behind. Since the bodies had been moved and cleaned, it was hard to tell if that was still the case. But based on that wound, it looked like it had been a stroke from right to left. Perhaps the killer had grabbed each victim by the back of their hair with their right hand, and then slit their throats with his left.

A left-handed killer?

Feeling sick to her stomach, she turned away from the dead girls.

"Thank you," she said to the coroner. "You've been very helpful."

"Not a problem," he replied, looking at the bodies. "I hope you catch the guy who did this. I'd hate to see another young woman like this on my table."

Taylor nodded, and then she and Wesley left the morgue, letting the heavy door shut behind them. She couldn't draw any concrete conclusions yet—she needed to get back to HQ and do more research.

CHAPTER SEVEN

Back at Quantico, Taylor sat in the briefing room with her laptop open in front of her, an empty cup of coffee beside her. Wesley was out grabbing more while Taylor had the file for the first victim—Emily Johnson—open in front of her.

As far as Taylor could tell, there was no connection between Mary and Emily other than the ages. Emily was twenty-four, Mary twenty-six. But they looked very different. Mary had brown hair and blue eyes. Emily had blonde hair and brown eyes. Mary had worked in a flower shop. Emily was a bartender.

But like Mary, Emily had been killed in an alleyway. While Mary's had been beside a toy shop, Emily's happened beside an apartment building. One commercial alleyway, one residential. Taylor scrolled through the file, unsure what to make of all this.

She leaned back in her chair and glanced at her phone, face-down on the table. She chewed on her lip before she couldn't resist anymore. She checked the phone. Still no call about Angie.

I should just give them one quick call, Taylor thought. But something in her hesitated. She knew she'd get a call when Angie was awake, and she didn't want to be too pushy. Plus, she was on a case. She needed to focus.

But at the same time, Taylor had waited two decades to see her sister again, and she wanted nothing more than to go be with her. To talk to her. This anxiety was like nothing she'd ever felt before. She figured once she'd saved Angie, everything would just suddenly be solved, but now she was dealing with more nerves than ever before.

Taylor was about to pick up the phone, just as Wesley came back into the room holding two coffees and a paper bag under his arm. Taylor pulled her hand away.

"Hey," Wesley said, setting the coffee in front of Taylor and taking a seat. He slid the paper bag over to her. "Bagel?"

"Thanks," Taylor said, accepting the coffee and food.

"So," Wesley asked, unwrapping his sandwich, "you find anything new?"

"No." Taylor shook her head. "Nothing."

She opened the bag and took out a bagel. She stared at it for a moment before she took a bite. The salty flavor made her feel better. And it was real food. She'd probably make herself sick eating too quickly, but at the moment she didn't care. She needed something to keep her going.

"The victims don't seem to have any connection," Taylor said, wiping her mouth with a napkin. "They lived at opposite ends of the city. They have nothing in common besides the fact that they were killed."

"That's true," Wesley agreed. He took a big bite of his sandwich, chewed, and then continued. "But the killer must have some sort of connection with them. He chose them, right? So they must have some sort of link."

"Maybe," Taylor said. She shrugged and took another bite of her bagel. "I'm not sure."

"Well, we need to figure it out," Wesley said. He leaned back in his chair and took a sip of his coffee. "Because if we don't, more people are going to die."

Taylor was well aware of that, but she was stumped.

She looked back at her computer screen. But she could feel Wesley's eyes on her. She looked up, meeting his gaze. He didn't look away.

"What is it?" she asked him.

He paused, looked away for a moment, then said, "I'm just wondering if you're okay."

"What do you mean?" she asked, a bit taken aback.

"I mean, about your sister," Wesley said. "You haven't seen her in years. And now she's in the hospital. I'm just wondering if you're holding up okay on a personal level."

Taylor stared at him for a long moment. Was she okay? She wasn't sure. Part of her was burying things and just trying to focus on work. "I'm fine," she said. But even as she said the words, she knew they weren't true.

She was far from fine. She was worried about Angie and feeling guilty that she wasn't there with her. But she had a job to do, and she couldn't let her personal life get in the way of that.

"Sorry," Wesley said. "I didn't mean to pry."

"It's okay," Taylor said. She forced a smile and went back to her computer screen. "I appreciate your concern, Wes."

It was nice to know that someone was looking out for her. Especially when she felt like she was falling apart. One part of her just wanted to work—the other part wanted to rip out of here and go see her sister. She was so close to having her normal life back. Her normal family.

They could have dinners at the dining room table again. Taylor wondered if the dark part of the turkey would still be Angie's favorite. If she still loved to mix her cranberry sauce with her mashed potatoes. Taylor had always found that so weird and gross, but Angie had loved it.

Taylor longed for those days. Normalcy. It was something she hadn't had in a long time. And now it was within her reach, but it felt so far away.

Taylor remembered one year on Thanksgiving, Angie had convinced Taylor to try the mashup too. She'd been about nine, and she'd pestered Taylor until Taylor finally gave in. Not just to avoid the pestering, but because she secretly kind of wanted to know how it tasted too.

Taylor still remembered how it had felt the first time it had hit her tongue. It was completely disgusting. But she'd smiled and tried her hardest to hide it. She didn't want to hurt Angie's feelings. And besides, that year, they'd all been really happy together in their little family of four. And to Taylor, that was all that mattered.

Her family was her top priority. She couldn't fail Angie. She had to be there for her.

But she couldn't be here and there at the same time.

She had to work.

"Anyway," Taylor said, "I know we have nothing so far, but maybe we should brainstorm a profile for this guy."

"Good idea," Wesley said. He grabbed the rest of his sandwich and took another bite. Then he picked up a Post-it Note and started writing. "Okay, so we're looking for a guy, right?"

"Right," Taylor said.

"And he's killed two people so far," Wesley stated. He finished his sandwich and bunched up the wrapper. "So the M.O. is to slit the victim's throat, and then he—" Wesley paused. "What do you think the killer does to them?"

Taylor had thought about that. She'd seen a lot of crime scenes. Sometimes they were staged, to make some sort of statement. Other times, they were more sinister; there would be evidence of assault, or sexual motives for a crime. But this one didn't seem to have any motive at all.

"I don't know, to tell you the truth," Taylor said. "I don't see any evidence of assault or rape. So I'd assume that he's just killing them… for the sake of it."

"So he's killing them and then he's leaving them. Did he take anything from them?"

"No," Taylor said. "Nothing was taken. It doesn't look like he went through their pockets or removed any jewelry or anything."

"Okay," Wesley said, writing that down too. "So I guess he's just killing them to kill them."

"Seems that way," Taylor said. "But I think we should assume he isn't done yet."

One thing was certain: the women in Flyway City were not safe. How could Taylor ensure no one else was hurt, when she didn't have a single clue who she was chasing?

Then an idea occurred to her. If they couldn't find the killer, but they knew he was out there, targeting women after dark, then there was one thing they could do to at least help prevent more lives being lost.

"Wesley," Taylor said, "I think we should get the Flyway PD to put out a citywide warning for women to not be alone after dark."

He looked up at her, eyebrows raised in surprise. "You think that's necessary?"

"I do," Taylor said. "This guy is targeting women, and we have no idea who he is or why he's doing it. If we can warn people and help them take precautions, maybe we can stop him before he hurts anyone else."

Wesley nodded. "Okay," he said. "I'll make the call."

A few minutes later and Wesley was on the phone with the Flyway Police Department. He was relaying Taylor's request to the captain, but Taylor thought he had the captain on his side, because it sounded like Wesley didn't have to put up much of a fight.

"Okay, great," Wesley said into the phone. "You'll cooperate? I'm glad to hear it. Thanks, Captain Rogers."

Taylor wished more people were like that. It sounded like this Captain Rogers had a level head, and he knew that there were no more urgent cases than this one. So far, the Flyway PD had been more cooperative with the FBI than some police forces Taylor had worked with in her time.

When Wesley finished the call, he hung up the phone and turned to Taylor. "Good news," he said. "He's putting out a warning for women to not go out alone after dark. He's going to put it on the police station's website, and he'll send the statement out through social media."

"Oh, good," Taylor said. "That should help." She leaned back in her chair. "I hope it helps."

If it didn't, then another young girl would surely die soon.

CHAPTER EIGHT

The street was too crowded, making his brain buzz with anxious thoughts. They were all looking at him. They could all see him—hear him, even though he'd never uttered a word to anyone. Not in years.

He kept his head low as he ducked through the busy sidewalk, past businesses and homeless people begging for change. Pathetic. He hated being out. He hated seeing so many filthy people in one place.

But he was going somewhere. Somewhere important to him. A place from his past…

He'd never tell.

There was a traffic light ahead. He crossed the street, walking past a Chinese food stand and several people who were asking for money. He kept his head low, trying to avoid their gaze. One man looked at another homeless man and said, "Get a job, bum."

He ignored the people around him and dug his hands deeper into his pockets. He could feel the rough fabric of his jacket against his skin and the cold metal of loose change in his pocket. He kept walking, moving down the street. The sound of his shoes against the pavement was drowned out by the sound of traffic and the hustle and bustle of the city. He accidentally bumped into someone's shoulder. A man, who was at least a head and shoulders taller than him, looked down at him and scowled. The man had a beard that was long and unkempt. His eyes were a cold, hard blue. He was wearing a worn-out leather jacket and dirty jeans.

"Watch where you're going," the man said.

The sharp words cut through him and he quickened his pace, head still down. He was getting close now. He could feel it. The memories were just on the edge of his mind, taunting him.

He turned down a side street and then another, until he was in front of the building. The museum with the American flags flapping in the wind. It looked just like he remembered it. His heart constricted in his chest as he stared at it.

It had been so long since he'd been here. Too long.

His fists clenched as he remembered the day his father had taken him here, all those years ago, back when he had a voice.

He remembered his father's words. *You sound like a pansy, you gross little shit! Don't talk—you're embarrassing me!*

His father had dragged him out of the museum and through the crowd of people onto the street. He'd sobbed, tears streaming down his cheeks, feeling like the ugliest, most unlovable thing in the world. But he hadn't said a word.

You're a little freak! his father had said.

He stood there on the sidewalk and listened to his father's footsteps as they faded away. He had never felt so alone in his whole life. Not until now.

He took in a breath of the afternoon air and sighed. He was alone… but soon, he'd have a friend again.

CHAPTER NINE

In the briefing room at Quantico, Taylor could feel her eyelids growing heavier by the moment. She was still sitting there with Wesley, still with her laptop out, trying to find a connection between the two victims—because she just didn't know what else to do. If it was a crime of opportunity, then there could be nothing linking them at all. But something in Taylor's gut told her to look just a little deeper, just in case there was a reason why these two young women shared the same fate.

She accidentally let out a yawn. She realized then that she hadn't slept in over twenty-four hours. Not even a nap. Taylor was getting really tired. Her eyes felt like they were made of sand, and every time she blinked, it felt like tiny needles were scraping against her eyeballs. She knew she needed to sleep, but she just couldn't bring herself to do it. Not yet. There was still too much work to be done.

But letting that yawn slip had clearly alerted Wesley, because he said, "Taylor, why don't you take a break? Get some sleep. I'll keep working on this."

"No, I'm okay," Taylor said, stifling another yawn. "I just need to find the connection between these two victims. There has to be something that links them together."

The files had yielded no results, so Taylor had turned her search to social media. She had both Emily's and Mary's profiles open. Emily's profile showed a woman who liked to have fun. She was always smiling in her photos and there were lots of pictures of her with her friends. In many of them, she was holding a drink.

Mary's profile, on the other hand, was much more subdued. There were few pictures of her smiling and most of them were taken at work.

Taylor scrolled through both profiles, looking for anything that might be a clue.

And then she saw it.

Mary had checked in at a place called Free Spirit Pilates. The name stood out to Taylor, and she quickly went back to the tab containing Emily's social media profile.

Emily had checked in at Free Spirit Pilates too.

Taylor's heart jolted in her chest. This was it. This was the connection.

"I know that look," Wesley said. "What have you got, Sage?"

"I just checked something on Mary's profile," Taylor said. "She checked in at the same place as Emily, Free Spirit Pilates."

"Damn," Wesley said. "That's a hell of a coincidence if it isn't the connection."

Taylor stood up, slamming her laptop. Finally: a lead. "Let's go pay them a visit."

***

Taylor shifted in the seat of Wesley's car as they pulled up to the building. It was a small studio with a sign that read "Free Spirit Pilates." The parking lot was full of cars, and there were people milling about outside the building. The studio looked busy, but not too crowded. Taylor could see people inside the studio, moving about and chatting. The atmosphere was friendly and relaxed.

As soon as they walked in, they were greeted by a petite woman wearing yoga pants and a tank top. She had her hair pulled back in a messy bun and she was sweating slightly. Her skin was flushed and her eyes were bright. She looked like she had just finished a workout. She looked like she was in a hurry, but she still took the time to greet them warmly.

"Can I help you?" she asked.

Taylor flashed her badge, and Wesley did the same. "We're with the FBI," Taylor said. "Are you the instructor?"

Her eyebrows went up. "I am—I'm Carrie."

"We're looking for information on two of your students," Taylor said. "Emily Johnson and Mary Gibbons."

The woman's face softened slightly. "I'm so sorry to hear about what happened to them. They were both great students."

"Do you know if they had any enemies?" Wesley asked. "Anyone who might have wanted to hurt them?"

"Not specifically, no…" She looked over her shoulder. It looked like a class had just finished up, as a group of women were walking through the lobby to leave. Carrie leaned closer to Taylor and Wesley and said, "Well, here's the thing. I don't want to scare off my customers, so please keep it down."

The two agents nodded, but Taylor's ears perked. Whatever this was could be helpful, and jolts of adrenaline went through her.

"There's been a man who's been coming here and watching the women during their classes," Carrie said. "He never says anything, he just watches. I've tried to confront him, but he always leaves before I can get close enough to talk to him."

That sounded promising. A creep lurking on women, where two women were now dead? Taylor needed to know more.

"Do you have any idea who he is?" Taylor asked.

Carrie shook her head. "No, I've never seen him before. But I got a good look at his car once. It's an old black sedan. I remember because it's pretty beat up."

"Can you tell us what he looks like?" Wesley asked.

"I don't know…I don't want to get anyone in trouble." Carrie looked over her shoulder again, as if she was worried someone would overhear them.

"It's okay," Taylor said soothingly. "We just want to talk to him. We're not going to do anything to him unless we have to."

"Okay, well… I remember what he looks like. He's tall and thin, with dark hair. He always wears a black jacket. I could be wrong, but I'm pretty sure I heard one of the women say he tried to hit on them, and introduced himself as Greg."

"That's helpful," Taylor said. "Can you think of anything else that might be useful?"

Carrie thought for a moment. "Well, I remember that Emily and Mary were both in the early morning class on Tuesday mornings."

So maybe that was when he'd hunted them, Taylor thought.

"Anything else?" Taylor prompted. Her pulse was pounding fast. This could be a real lead. If the guy was coming here to select targets, then that could be a huge break in the investigation. At least, she hoped it would be.

"No, that's all I can think of," Carrie said. "I'm sorry I couldn't be more help."

"Don't worry about it," Taylor said. "You did great. Anything you remember could be helpful. Thank you so much for your time."

"Of course," Carrie said. "I'm so sorry about what happened. If there's anything I can do, please don't hesitate to ask."

"We may need you to come in and make an official statement," Wesley told her. "But for now, we'll just take it from here."

"Sounds good," Carrie said. "Just do me a favor and be careful, okay? I don't want anyone else to get hurt."

"I will," Wesley promised. "We'll be in touch."

The two agents walked out of the building and back to their car. Taylor had her phone out and was already dialing Detective Reynolds before they even got in their seats.

"I hope you're calling to tell me you found the unsub," Reynolds said. "I wasn't a fan of my case being taken over by the feds, but whatever gets the job done." His words were passive-aggressive, but his tone was jovial, so Taylor got the sense he was just joking around. For all intents and purposes, Reynolds seemed like a good guy and an honest cop.

"Not quite," Taylor said. "Actually, I was hoping you might have information on a potential suspect."

"Oh? How can I help?"

"We've got a name," Taylor said. "His name is Greg, and he's been hitting on women at this Pilates studio."

"If it's the same Greg I'm thinking of, he's been on our radar for a while," Reynolds said. "He's a real sleazeball. We've gotten complaints from several women about him harassing them, making lewd comments, following them home. He's been warned numerous times, but he just doesn't seem to get the message."

"Do you think he could be our unsub?" Taylor asked. It certainly sounded like he fit the profile.

"It's possible," Reynolds said. "We haven't been able to pin anything on him yet, but I wouldn't put it past him. He's a real creep."

"What do you know about him?" Taylor asked.

"Not much," Reynolds said. "He's originally from out of state, but he moved here about five years ago. We don't have any family or friends listed for him. He works odd jobs here and there, but nothing steady."

That could easily fit the profile.

"We need to bring him in for questioning," Taylor said. "Can you tell me where to find him?"

"Roger that," Reynolds said. "I'll send you the address."

"Thanks, Detective." Taylor paused. "And for what it's worth, we appreciate you cooperating with us on this case. I know it's not always easy to step aside."

Reynolds grunted on the other end of the phone. "All good. Just promise me you'll nail this guy. Or I will."

Taylor smiled. "You got it."

"Sending the address now."

With that, Taylor hung up. If this Greg guy was behind the murders, then he wouldn't get away with it. Not on Taylor's watch.

CHAPTER TEN

Wesley had a bad feeling about this.

He and Taylor had just arrived at the perp's—Greg's—house, and it was definitely not a sight for sore eyes. The house was small and run-down, with peeling paint and a rickety porch. The yard was overgrown with weeds and there was a car up on blocks in the driveway. He could hear Taylor muttering to herself as she took in the sight. "What a dump," she said. "No wonder the guy went off the rails."

"Well, we better be careful," Wesley said. "We don't know what this guy is like."

Whenever he worked with Taylor Sage, trouble—and violence—seemed to follow them. They'd had more than a few perps lose their minds on them, and Wesley didn't want to take any chances. Taylor was going through enough with her family; the last thing he wanted was for her to get hurt working a case.

Wesley knocked on the door, but there was no answer. He tried again, but still nothing. "Greg Bean, this is the FBI. If you're in there, open up!"

No answer.

"I don't think anyone's home," Taylor said. She paused for a moment, considering what to do next. "Let's look around back."

Following Taylor's lead, Wesley made his way around the side of the house, being careful to stay low and out of sight. He didn't want to give Greg any reason to start shooting if he was in there. He got to the back of the house. "Hey, Sage," he called softly. "I found an open window."

He climbed the steps up to the porch and went to the window. He paused for a moment, listening for any movement inside the house. A rotten smell wafted out, and Wesley could see that the kitchen sink was swarming with fruit flies and other insects.

"It seems like he hasn't been home in a while," Wesley muttered.

Taylor was beside him now, and she scrunched her nose. "That smells like death… I wonder if he's in there…"

Wesley shot her a look. "What, you think he's dead in there?"

"It certainly smells like it." Taylor paused, chewing on her lip. "Let's go in."

"You sure?" Wesley raised a brow. He doubted the guy was a corpse in there—but then again, this window was wide open. Taylor nodded, so Wesley slowly lifted himself up and over the windowsill, being careful not to make too much noise.

He landed in a crouch on the floor and quickly scanned his surroundings. He looked around at the kitchen. It was small and cramped, with dirty dishes piled high in the sink. The counters were cluttered with empty food containers, and that smell grew even stronger. Maybe Taylor was right—maybe there was a corpse in here.

Taylor climbed in through the window after him, landing in the house with a soft thud. She pulled out her gun and gestured for Wesley to go first. He nodded and slowly began making his way through the house. The place was dark and musty-smelling, with piles of clothes and garbage strewn about.

But when they got to the living room, Wesley spotted the source of the stink: there was an old rotisserie chicken sitting half-eaten on the coffee table, and it was so rotten it had maggots on it.

"Not exactly the corpse we were expecting," Wesley muttered. It took a lot to get his stomach churning, but this made even him want to throw up.

"So he's not dead," Taylor said. "We might as well look around while we're here."

Wesley nearly laughed. He knew the whole corpse thing was an excuse to get them in the house and poke around, and he wasn't opposed to it. This guy looked as dirty as his house smelled, and Wesley wouldn't be surprised at all if he had something to do with these girls.

They checked each room carefully, but there was no sign of Greg. It was as if the house was abandoned. Wesley was about to give up and go back outside when he noticed a calendar on the wall. It was covered in scribbled-out dates and random words. The date on the calendar was circled in red.

"Hey, Taylor," he said softly, pointing to the calendar. "Look at this."

"What is it?" Taylor asked, coming up behind him.

"Look."

On today's date, circled in red, it said YOGA DAY.

Wesley exchanged a perplexed look with Taylor. But he could see the gears clinking in her head.

"This must be his plan," Taylor said. "He's probably at a yoga studio right now, scoping for another victim."

Wesley's stomach turned. He knew she was right. They had to find Greg and stop him before he could hurt anyone else.

Wesley took out his phone and searched for the nearest yoga studio. "There's a studio ten minutes from here," he said, his heart pounding.

Taylor nodded. Her eyes were steely with determination. "Let's go."

***

Wesley and Taylor arrived at the yoga studio to find an ongoing class. The room was filled with people in various yoga poses, their bodies stretching and contorting in ways that seemed impossible. Wesley scanned the room for Greg, but he didn't see him anywhere. The class was in full swing, with people flowing from one pose to the next. The room was heated, and the air was thick with the smell of sweat and determination. The people were of all shapes and sizes, but they all had one thing in common: they were all completely focused on their practice.

"Do you see him?" Taylor whispered.

Wesley shook his head. "No, but he could be hiding somewhere. Maybe he saw us come in."

They split up and began checking around the studio.

It was difficult to move through the room while staying unnoticed. Wesley kept his eyes open, looking for any sign of Greg. He let his eyes wander over each person, searching for a sign of wrongdoing. But he didn't see a thing.

All of a sudden, a woman's voice boomed through the room. "That's it for this class. Remember to breathe and leave your worries at the door."

The room began to clear out, and Taylor walked back over to Wesley. They watched as the people filed out, their muscles still glowing from the workout.

Wesley surveyed the room. "Any sign of him?"

"No." Taylor's voice shook with frustration. "It's like he just disappeared."

"This whole place is weird," Wesley said, his voice hushed. "It's like something out of a sixties hippie movie."

"I know what you mean," Taylor said. "And everyone seems so…happy."

They gained some confused looks from people as they passed them—everyone was dressed to work out while Wesley was wearing a casual suit, and Taylor was in a blouse with black pants. They looked like FBI agents. If Greg had seen them, he was probably either hiding or had already escaped. Damn.

If he was hiding, then Wesley had a good idea where he might be.

"There's one more place I gotta check," Wesley said. "You keep looking."

With that, Wesley took off. He checked the men's bathroom, but there was no sign of Greg. He was about to leave when he heard a noise coming from one of the stalls. It sounded like someone was trying to stifle a cry. He slowly approached the stall and kicked the door open. Greg was inside, huddled in the corner. He was shaking and his eyes were wide with fear.

He looked up at Wesley.

"Please don't kill me," he begged.

"Stand up," Wesley ordered. Greg slowly got to his feet, his hands shaking uncontrollably. "Turn around. Are you Greg Bean?"

"Yes, but—I was just looking around, I—"

Before Wesley could even blink, Greg shoved him back and scrambled as fast as he could toward the exit. *Son of a bitch!* Greg darted into the yoga studio, and Wesley barreled after him.

Wesley and Taylor both sprinted after Greg as he darted through the yoga studio. He was surprisingly fast for a man of his size, and he was quickly gaining ground. They could hear his footsteps pounding against the floor, echoing through the room.

Another class was beginning, and the new people in the studio were still stretched out in various yoga poses, completely oblivious to the chase that was happening right in front of them. Wesley and Taylor weaved in and out of the sea of bodies, and Wesley's heart pounded in his chest. He didn't realize he'd be getting so much cardio in today.

Greg reached the exit and pushed his way through the door, nearly knocking a woman over in the process. Wesley and Taylor were right behind him as he sprinted down the street. They could see his broad back as he pumped his arms furiously, powering himself forward.

Wesley was gaining on Greg, but he was still too far ahead. Taylor put on a burst of speed and leapt forward, tackling Greg to the ground.

"Get off me!" Greg shouted, struggling to break free.

Taylor quickly pinned him down.

"Stop struggling," she said, trying to keep her voice calm and even. "It's over."

Greg stopped fighting and Wesley helped Taylor hold him still. They stood up, and Taylor pulled out her handcuffs. She began to cuff his hands behind his back.

"Did you really think you could get away with it?" Taylor said. She was trying to keep her voice calm, but Wesley could hear the anger bubbling up inside of her. "Did you think we wouldn't catch you?"

"You can't do this to me," Greg said. "I'm not a criminal."

"We can do whatever we want," Wesley said, his voice cold. "You broke the law."

"I'm innocent," Greg said, but his voice was pleading, not confident. "You're making a mistake."

"No," Taylor said. "You're the one who's made the mistake. You shouldn't have hurt those people."

"Hurt people? I didn't, I—I was just looking, I swear!"

Taylor shoved him forward. "Save it, Greg. We know what you've been up to."

They dragged him down the street, gaining looks from people, but Wesley kept his posture firm.

They'd nailed him.

And Wesley knew that Greg knew it too. His face had gone pale and he was sweating profusely.

"This is wrong," Greg said. "You aren't supposed to do this. It's not right."

Wesley and Taylor exchanged a look, but they didn't say anything. Instead, they continued to lead him onward.

CHAPTER ELEVEN

Taylor took her seat, ready to get the truth. The interrogation room looked like any other interrogation room: white walls, a table with a few chairs, and a two-way mirror. Greg was sitting at the table, his hands cuffed together, his head hung in shame. Wesley took his spot beside Taylor.

"So, Greg," Taylor began. "Can you tell me what you were doing at the yoga studio?"

"I was just looking around," Greg said. His voice was small and weak, and Taylor couldn't help but think of him as pathetic. She hated men like this—men who objectified women, made them uncomfortable by creeping on them and looking at them too much. It all made her sick.

"Just looking around?" Taylor raised an eyebrow. "It looked to us like you were trying to escape."

"I wasn't trying to escape," Greg said. "I was just using the bathroom..."

"Why were you trying to get away from us?" Taylor asked. "What were you doing that you didn't want us to see?"

Greg swallowed hard and shook his head. "I don't know what you're talking about."

"Come on, Greg," Taylor said. "We know what you've been up to. We know you've been following women."

"What? No, I haven't been following anyone!" Greg protested.

"We have witnesses who saw you following them," Wesley added in. "You can't escape this, Greg."

"I'm innocent! I swear!"

Taylor took a breath. She didn't want to waste any time on this guy—he was clearly unhinged. And he just might be their killer. Taylor took out a photo of Mary Gibbons and slapped it on the table. She slid it toward Greg.

"Do you recognize this woman?"

Greg hesitated before looking down at the photo. His eyes widened as he stared at it.

"Don't play dumb," Wesley said. "Tell us what you know."

He gulped. "Yes," he said, his voice barely a whisper.

"Did you follow her?" Taylor asked.

"Yes," he admitted, his head low. "I did. But—I never talked to her, I just thought she was pretty."

"Bullshit," Wesley said. "You attacked her, didn't you, Greg?"

"No!" Greg said, his voice desperate. "I didn't do anything like that!"

"Don't lie to us, Greg," Taylor said, her voice serious. "We're here to find out the truth, and the sooner you're honest with us, the better this will go for you."

"I didn't do anything!" Greg shouted. Desperation was clearly in his voice. "I just liked to watch her. That's all."

Taylor and Wesley exchanged a look. Taylor wasn't buying it.

"Greg," Taylor said, "this woman is Mary Gibbons. She was found dead this morning."

Greg went pale. "W-what? And you think *I* did it?"

"Did you?" Taylor's eyes hardened on Greg. He was going to have to be more convincing than that if he wanted her to believe he was innocent. He just shook his head violently, and Taylor pulled out another photo, this one of Emily Johnson. "What about this woman, Greg? You recognize her, don't you?"

"I, I—" He looked down at the photo, but couldn't finish his sentence. But Taylor had what she needed.

"You recognize both of these women, Greg," Taylor said, "because you killed them."

"No!" Greg shouted. "I didn't kill anyone!"

"You were seen at the Pilates studio both of these women attended," Wesley said.

"That doesn't mean I did it!" Greg protested. "I used to go there and just watch them sometimes, okay? But I'd never hurt anyone. I'd never act… please, you have to believe me!" Greg pleaded. "I didn't do it! I have an alibi!"

Taylor paused and glanced at Wesley. If he really did have an alibi, then that would clear him—and this would be a dead end. Taylor gritted her teeth as she stared into Greg's eyes. He looked like a piece of shit, and he was clearly a pervert.

But if he wasn't the killer, then that would mean the real killer was still out there—likely stalking his next victim.

"What's your alibi, Greg?" Taylor asked, her voice hard. "If you didn't do it, then you need to tell us where you were."

“I was with someone,” Greg said, his voice quiet. “I-I was with someone the entire time.”

“Who was it?” Wesley asked.

“Well, it was my coworker,” he said. “We were gaming and getting drunk all night. We passed out on the couch at his place. I never left. I swear, I didn’t hurt anyone.”

Taylor considered that for a moment. It was possible that Greg was telling the truth and he wasn’t the killer. But she still didn’t like him. He was a creep who had been stalking Mary and Emily. Even if he hadn’t killed them, he was still guilty of something.

“We’re going to have to look into this, Greg,” Taylor said. “I’m going to have to check with your coworker to make sure this is true.”

“Of course it’s true!” Greg said. “I’d never lie about something like this! I’m innocent, I promise.”

“I’m going to talk to your friend, Greg,” Taylor said. “What’s his name?”

“It’s Ethan,” Greg said. “Ethan Winters. I can give you his information.” He rattled off Ethan’s address and phone number.

“Thank you, Greg,” Taylor said. “We’ll be in touch. Until then, you can sit here and think about how uncomfortable you’ve made all the women you’ve been gawking at.”

“You can’t just leave me here!” Greg exclaimed as Taylor and Wesley went for the exit.

Taylor took one last look at him before she left, slamming the door behind her.

CHAPTER TWELVE

Taylor paced the sidewalk outside of the Flyway police station, the sky dark now. It was getting cold, and the wind cut through her blouse. She hugged herself, but inside, she was steaming with frustration.

Greg's alibi had checked out. The coworker vouched for him. And even had video evidence of him and Greg livestreaming the video game they were playing—so they really were together.

Greg Bean was a dead end.

"Damn it," Taylor said.

Wesley came up behind her. "Hey, it was a good lead," he said.

"Yeah, but it's a dead end," Taylor said. "We're still looking for the killer." She sighed. "Where do we go from here?"

Wesley shrugged. "We can always go back to the victims' houses," he said. "Maybe we missed something."

"Maybe…" Taylor sighed. She wasn't feeling optimistic, and plus, the fact that she hadn't slept was starting to wear on her. Her eyelids felt heavy, and her mind wasn't working at full capacity. She took out her phone.

Taylor's heart skipped a beat as she saw a missed call from the hospital. She quickly called back, her mind racing with worry and hope. Wesley stood back.

"Hello?" a nurse answered.

"Hi, this is Taylor Sage," Taylor said. "I'm Angela Sage's sister. I missed a call from you."

"Oh, yes," the nurse said. "Angie woke up earlier, but she was… very agitated. We had to sedate her again."

"Is she alright?" Taylor asked, her heart racing. What did she mean "agitated"?

"She's stable for now," the nurse said. "But we'll have to keep an eye on her. She's currently asleep again, so I'm afraid we don't have much news to share."

Taylor's heart sank. This was all too much.

"Thank you," she barely managed to say, then hung up. She felt defeated.

Taylor felt like she was going to collapse. Her legs felt like lead, and her head was swimming. She swayed on the spot, and Wesley rushed over to catch her.

"Hey, are you okay?" he asked, worry etched into his features. "Sage, you're as white as a sheet."

"I'm fine," Taylor lied. She wasn't fine. She was tired, frustrated, and worried about her sister. But she had to keep it together. There was still work to be done.

"Let's get you home," Wesley said. "You need some rest."

"No," Taylor said firmly. "I can't go home now. We're still working."

"Taylor," Wesley said gently. "You're exhausted. You need to sleep."

"No," Taylor repeated, more forcefully this time. "I can't stop now. Those women need my help."

"Sage…" Wesley sighed. Above them, the stars were emerging, and there were only a few cars passing by on the quiet street. Taylor knew she was being stubborn. But it was in her nature. "All the women have been warned to stay inside, okay?" Wesley said. "There's no sense in hurting yourself just to keep working. At the very least, let's find a hotel. Then you'll be in town to keep working right away once you've had some rest."

Taylor thought about it for a moment. She knew she was being overly stubborn and that Wesley was just looking out for her. And he was right, too. She was tired, and she wasn't on top of her game.

"That's… that's a good idea," Taylor said. She was still trying to convince herself that she wasn't going to be able to do anything at this point. She needed to sleep. "Let's find a hotel."

Wesley took out his phone to look for one. Taylor leaned against the police station wall and took a deep breath, sighing in frustration. Her mind was foggy, and she wasn't sure if it was the stress or the lack of sleep that was making her feel this way. She had a pounding headache and her eyelids felt like they were made of lead.

Wesley returned a few moments later. He ran his hands through his black hair, and Taylor noticed that his eyes were tired too. "I found one not too far away," he said. "C'mon. I'll drive us."

"Thanks," Taylor said. She walked down the road with Wesley, leaning heavily on him. Her body felt lethargic, and the cold air was starting to get to her. She stopped and turned to Wesley. "I never thought I'd be this person," she said softly. Normally, she could keep going. Even on little sleep. But it was getting so hard, and she felt so heavy.

Wesley's gray eyes were warm, warmer than they usually were. "You'll feel better once you get some rest," he said. "Come on."

Taylor wasn't sure if she was imagining it, but something between them felt different.

She really did need some sleep.

***

In the lobby of the hotel, Taylor fought to keep her head upright as Wesley talked to the receptionist. The desk was a large, imposing structure made of dark wood. It was polished to a shine, and the nameplate of the hotel was etched into the surface. The receptionist was a young woman with her hair pulled back in a tight bun. She was wearing a name tag that said "Jessica." Wesley leaned on the counter, his large body looking exhausted.

"What do you mean you only have one bed?" Wesley asked. "I booked this room for two people."

"I'm terribly sorry," Jessica said, not sounding terribly sorry at all. "We were completely booked up this weekend. There were a lot more people in town than we'd anticipated. But you're welcome to check out any other hotel in the area."

"There are no other hotels," Taylor muttered. Wesley glanced at her, but Jessica didn't seem to hear.

"That's not acceptable," Wesley said. "We reserved a room with two beds, not one."

"I understand," Jessica said. "But we were completely booked for this weekend, and whoever talked to you on the phone must have misunderstood."

Wesley looked agitated, his face flushed and his neck dotted with red, but Taylor was too tired to care; she could sleep on the floor if she had to.

"Wes," Taylor said tiredly, "there's no point in arguing with her. We're just going to have to deal with it."

"You sure?" he asked, raising a thick eyebrow. "You're not uncomfortable?"

"Why would I be?"

A moment of silence spread between them. Taylor realized what Wesley was getting at. But they were partners—it wasn't a big deal.

That was what Taylor told herself, even though she had to admit that the thought of being in the same bed with Wesley all night had her feeling… nervous.

Jessica blinked. "So, should I…?"

"We'll take it," Wesley said.

"Just make sure the room is clean." He pulled out his wallet and pulled out a few bills, which he put on the desk.

"Of course," Jessica said. "I'll get the key for you."

She disappeared into the back room, then came back moments later with a keycard. "Room 304," she said.

Wesley took the keycard and Taylor followed him to the elevator. They got in, and Wesley hit the button for the third floor. The doors closed with a soft ding, and they were whisked up to their floor.

The hallway was dimly lit, and their room was at the end of it. Wesley put the keycard in the door and pushed it open. He gestured for Taylor to go in first.

She did, and found that the room was small but clean. There was a queen-sized bed against one wall, a dresser on the other side of the room, and a small table with two chairs near the window. The carpet was deep burgundy, and there were white curtains pulled across the window.

"It's not exactly what we'd planned," Wesley said apologetically, "but it'll do."

Taylor turned to him. "It's perfect," she said. And she meant it—she didn't mind if they were too close. They'd make it work.

Wesley ran his hand along the back of his neck. "Was hoping there'd be a couch or something, but… I can take the floor."

"No way," Taylor said. "I'm not making you sleep on the floor."

"I don't mind," Wesley said. "It's not a big deal."

"No, seriously, Wes. We'll share the bed." She knew it was a crazy idea, even as she said it, but Taylor wasn't about to be responsible for her partner getting hurt in action because he had a bad back. The bed was huge. They would fit.

Wesley hesitated for a moment, then nodded. "All right."

He started to unpack his bag, and Taylor did the same. She put her clothes in the dresser, and Wesley put his in one of the drawers too.

"I'm gonna take a shower quick," Taylor said. She turned back to see Wesley's back facing her as he slid his shirt off. She tried not to stare at his body—broad shoulders, muscled chest, slim waist—but she couldn't help it. She hadn't been this close to a man since she and Ben broke up, and she felt her cheeks flush with heat.

"I'll see what channels this thing has," Wesley said, not looking at her.

Taylor slipped into the bathroom and closed the door behind her, sweatpants in hand. She always had a bag with her in case she had to stay overnight somewhere, but her essentials were basic. She'd never had to share a room with a partner before.

Taking a breath, Taylor turned on the shower.

She undressed quickly and got in, letting the hot water wash over her. It felt good to be clean, and she scrubbed her skin vigorously with the soap. She tried not to think about Wesley being in the other room, but she couldn't help it. Taylor didn't know what had changed between them, but she suddenly felt drawn to him, and acutely aware of his physical attractiveness.

It wasn't like she had any plans of being with anyone anytime soon. She hadn't even thought about men since the divorce from Ben. It was still in the process of being finalized. They'd been married for four years, and though their relationship had been rocky for a while, she never thought he would leave her. But he did.

Taylor's hand stilled on her stomach as she remembered the day he told her it was over. Even more painful were the memories of when she once wanted a child. Now, she knew, without a doubt, she would never have one. She wondered if she'd ever fall in love again. She wondered if her next partner would care whether she was infertile or not.

She thought about Wesley, in the other room again. He had a daughter. He seemed to love her more than anything in the world. Taylor admired that about him. As rough around the edges as he could be, he had a compassionate side, and Taylor could tell he was a good father.

Taylor felt a stirring deep inside of her that she hadn't felt in a long time. As the water ran down her body, she tried to shake the feeling away. She couldn't think like this about her partner. It would be completely unprofessional.

Belasco's reading from earlier slipped into her mind, intrusive, wiping away her other thoughts. She'd warned Taylor of a betrayal. Could it be Wesley? If Taylor did explore these feelings she had for him—could he break her heart?

After Ben, she wasn't sure if it were even possible to be hurt again. Maybe, if Wesley did break her heart, she'd just feel nothing. She wasn't sure. But the thought of it made her uneasy.

I shouldn't take Belasco so literally, she reminded herself. The tarot reader had warned her of a betrayal once before, back when Calvin Scott was her partner. But Calvin hadn't betrayed her—he'd just acted recklessly, resulting in him having to exit Taylor's life. So even if someone was going to "betray" her… it didn't mean it was literal. And besides, Taylor couldn't picture Wesley acting untrue.

She was getting ahead of herself anyway. They were partners—they weren't romantically involved.

Taylor got out of the shower and wrapped a towel around her body. She could hear the sound of the TV in the other room, and she knew Wesley was still up. She quickly dried off and then put on her sweatpants. She hesitated for a moment, then opened the door and walked out into the bedroom.

Wesley was sprawled on the bed, his head propped up on one hand as he watched the TV. He turned to look at her as she came in, and his eyes widened slightly at the sight of her with her hair wet, wearing sweatpants.

"Uh, sorry," he said, turning back to the TV. "Didn't mean to stare. Just not used to seeing you so casual."

"It's okay," Taylor said, feeling a little self-conscious. She went over to her bag and rummaged through it for her hair brush, which she ran through her silky black hair.

"Find anything good on TV?" she asked, hesitantly approaching the bed. The weight of exhaustion hit her again.

"Not really," Wesley said. "Just flipping through channels."

As she got closer to the bed, she could smell his cologne. It was a mix of sandalwood and citrus, and it made her stomach flutter. She stopped just inches from the bed and looked down at Wesley. He had the remote in his hand, and he was scrolling through the channels.

She could see the muscles in his arms as he shifted, and she felt her face flush with warmth. She hadn't been this close to a man in a long time. She didn't know what to do or say. All she wanted to do was reach out and touch him, feel those strong hands caress her skin.

But instead she said nothing and averted her gaze. She busied herself by gathering her things together, slowly putting them back into her bag. As she did so, she could feel Wesley's eyes on her, studying her every move.

Wesley focused back on the TV as Taylor got into the bed next to him, a safe distance away. The sheets were cool on her skin. Taylor rolled over onto her side, resting her head on her hand as she watched Wesley watch TV. She was exhausted, but something about being near him made her feel… safe.

She stretched out and closed her eyes.

A sleepy smile tugged at the corners of her lips. It felt good to be lying next to him, safe and warm. Even though she knew it was wrong to feel this way.

Taylor finally allowed herself to rest for the first time in what felt like days.

As she drifted off to sleep, she thought of Wesley, of the case, and of Angie.

CHAPTER THIRTEEN

Isabel smiled at her best friend, Francesca, as she stepped out of Francesca's house and into the cool October night. "Bye, Frannie! Thanks so much for having me!"

"Thank you so much for coming, Iz!" Francesca smiled, bright and warm.

"Don't mention it. I had a blast! And, of course, you know that I would never turn down a chance to party with you."

"Oh, I know. After all," Francesca said, her lip curving with an amused smile, "you can't party without me."

"I know! Although, even though I'm always the one getting drunk and falling on the floor, I have to wonder which one of us is actually more drunk."

"Always the quiet one, aren't you?" Francesca observed.

Isabel nodded, not disagreeing with her friend's comment. She had always been more reserved than Francesca. Maybe because she was older and had a bit more maturity than her younger, more carefree friend.

The two young women hugged again, before Isabel waved goodbye and walked down Francesca's driveway, onto the quiet suburb. The air was a bit cool for being October, and the moonless night made it difficult to see much. Still, something about the air, the freshness, the crispness sent relief throughout Isabel's body. She took off into the night, her footsteps quietly echoing onto the street.

Isabel had heard the warning on the news, cautioning women not to be outside alone in the dark, but Isabel's house was only a short walk away, and besides, this was her neighborhood—it was the safest neighborhood in the city, as far as she was concerned. They never even saw break-ins around here.

Isabel walked down her street, enjoying the cool autumn night. She was feeling so relaxed and happy, grateful for the chance to spend time with her best friend. Isabel had never felt so alive, so… complete.

Suddenly, a cold shiver ran down Isabel's spine. She stopped short, turning around to look behind her. Nothing was there. But she could feel someone watching her…

Okay, so maybe the police warning had gotten in her head a little more than she'd realized. Isabel started to feel uneasy, like someone was following her. She quickened her step, but still felt as if she were being watched.

Don't be ridiculous, she told herself. This is your home. *You grew up here. Nothing bad ever happens at home...*

Suddenly, something jumped out at Isabel and she twisted around to see nothing. She gasped and stumbled back a few steps, before regaining her composure and turning around again to continue on her way. Whatever had caused the sudden fear in Isabel's heart had already disappeared into the darkness.

It was nothing, she reasoned. When had she become so paranoid? This was a safe neighborhood. There was no reason to be so jumpy.

The fact that Isabel was partially deaf in one ear didn't help her anxiety, as sometimes she worried that if someone snuck up on her, she wouldn't be able to hear them properly. But she'd never encountered anything—or anyone—sinister before. Her house was only a short walk. She just needed to get there, then she'd feel better.

She kept walking down the street. And that was when she heard it:

"Help me..."

A child's voice.

What the heck? Had she heard that right? Maybe it was the wind. Assuming she'd just imagined it, she kept walking, but then:

"Help me..."

That child's voice again.

Isabel looked ahead.

Something was on the sidewalk.

Her heart began to pound. She kept walking, feeling fear course through her veins. At the same time, she couldn't stop.

In the middle of the sidewalk was a porcelain doll.

"Help... me..."

Isabel scowled. She wasn't sure what was going on here—but that voice. It hadn't come from the doll.

It had come from right behind her.

Isabel spun around—only to see a man standing there with a knife, gleaming in the light of the streetlamp.

He was coming right for her.

She screamed, sprinting as fast as she could down the street. She didn't know where she was going, only that she had to get away from him. She heard him behind her, his footsteps pounding on the pavement.

"Stop!" he yelled, still in that high-pitched voice.

The sound of his breathing was loud and furious, like a lion on the hunt. She could feel the tension in the air, like a storm brewing. Isabel ran as fast as she could, away from the man with the knife and into the night.

She saw a house with the lights on and ran straight for it. She banged violently on the door, screaming, "Help!" over and over again.

Isabel's heart was pounding so hard it hurt, and she could feel herself starting to hyperventilate. She stopped and leaned against the door for a moment, taking a deep breath.

The door began to open, and Isabel saw her neighbor Mrs. Sands standing there, a look of confusion on her face.

"Can I help you, dear?"

"He's right there! He's right there! Help me!" Isabel begged.

"What? Where?"

"He's right behind me!" Isabel said, closing her eyes and throwing her hands up in the air. "Help!"

Isabel pushed Mrs. Sands aside, grabbed her by the arm, and pulled her inside the house. She slammed the door shut and locked it.

"Isabel, sweetie, there was no one," Mrs. Sands said.

Isabel ran to the window and looked beyond the curtains, into the dark night.

The man wasn't there.

CHAPTER FOURTEEN

When Taylor walked into the hospital, the lights were all dark.

She didn't remember how she got here. It was like she was floating, her feet not even touching the pale white tiles of the hospital floor. But there was a door open up ahead. A light bled out from within.

Angie…

Angie was there.

It was like a beacon in the darkness, guiding her to safety. Taylor pushed the door open and stepped into the hospital room. Immediately, she felt a sense of relief wash over her.

Angie was awake!

The first thing that caught Taylor's eye was the intense light shining down on Angie from above. The second thing that caught her eye was the tear streaming down Angie's cheek.

"Hey," Taylor said softly, moving closer to the bed. "I'm here."

But Angie didn't look. With her long hair framing her pale face, her cheeks gaunt, she looked like a skeleton.

"Angie?" Taylor asked, her heart in her throat.

Slowly, she reached out to her sister—

Angie's eyes snapped to hers.

Taylor gasped.

"Who are you?" Angie asked.

"What? Angie, it's me, Taylor. I'm your sister."

But Angie didn't say anything else. Her eyes were dead, distant, and just stared at Taylor as she spoke.

"Angie," Taylor said, her voice cracking. "Come on. You know who I am. I'm your sister. Please. Please don't…"

But she trailed off, her voice falling to nothing. Taylor reached out to Angie's arm.

"No!" Angie shrieked. "Get away from me!"

Taylor backed away, her hand shaking. "Angie…please…I'm your sister," she said. "I'm your sister…"

"No… no… no…" Angie whispered.

"Angie?" Taylor asked, slowly making her way over to the bed. "Angie, are you okay?"

"NO!" Angie screamed. She began kicking and thrashing. With every movement, the hospital walls around them began to shake and crumble, until rubble was falling on Taylor's head.

She covered her face, trying to hide from the sheer devastation and noise.

She sobbed as she could barely stand.

"Angie! Angie! Angie, it's me, Taylor! It's me, it's Taylor. It's your little sister, and I'm here to save you."

It was like Angie no longer heard Taylor. She began to laugh.

"Angie…" Taylor said. "Angie, please…"

But Angie didn't respond. She continued laughing.

"Angie, please," Taylor said, grabbing her sister's legs. "Please don't. Angie, stop."

But Angie wasn't listening. She continued to thrash—

Until, finally, the hospital caught on fire.

And it all went black.

Taylor's eyes popped open, and she gasped for air as she came to. Wesley was holding her tight, his face inches from hers. She looked around; the room was dark and she could see nothing but blackness surrounding her.

"Wesley?" she said softly, trying to move away from him. "What's happening?"

"You were screaming," Wesley said gently. "I didn't know what to do."

Taylor shook her head, not understanding. The nightmare had been so real—so terrifying.

"It's okay," he said softly. "It's over now."

She nodded, blinking back tears as she tried to make sense of it all. It was just a dream. A dream about Angie.

But it had felt so real.

Taylor couldn't stop the tears from coming. In that moment, she lost all sensibility. She didn't think about the fact that Wesley, of all people, was holding her. All she could think about was the idea that when Angie woke up—she might not know who Taylor was anymore.

It had been two decades, after all. And when Taylor found Angie in that horrible cabin, Angie had looked at her like she was a ghost before she'd lost consciousness entirely.

Taylor's heart pounded in her chest as she tried to make sense of what was happening. She felt like she was going to faint—like the room was spinning and she couldn't breathe.

"Sage," Wesley said. His arms tightened around her, encasing her in his warmth. "It's okay. You're okay."

"I'm so sorry," Taylor said between breaths. "I'm such a mess. You shouldn't see me like this…"

"You're not. I've got you."

For just a moment, Taylor allowed herself to rest her head on his chest. His heart was beating fast. Taylor never thought she'd be close to a man like this, not after Ben. But it was all happening so fast.

She'd let him in, and now he was holding her.

Even if he was only holding her because she was being a mess.

Taylor pulled back, wiping her eyes and sniffing. Wesley had to let go of her to get a tissue. He began to wipe the tears from her cheeks.

"The nightmare is going to haunt me forever," Taylor said softly, her voice broken. "It felt so real. She… she woke up in this hospital and had no idea who I am…"

"That's not gonna happen," Wesley assured her. "You saved her, Sage, and she's your sister… she'll remember you. You've just gotta give her time."

Taylor's heart clenched. She hoped he was right.

Suddenly, Wesley's phone on the nightstand lit up, cutting into the darkness of the room. The digital clock next to it read 6:02 a.m.

So if someone was calling, it was probably work.

Wesley leaned over Taylor to reach the phone. "It's Winchester," he said, then answered. "This is Special Agent Wesley. What's going on?"

Taylor could hear Winchester's voice on the other end. "Wesley, you still with Sage?"

Wesley glanced down at Taylor, who shied away from him. They were so close. Hearing Winchester's voice grounded her back in reality.

"Yeah," Wesley said. "What's going on?"

A pause. "There's been another victim."

Taylor locked eyes with Wesley, her heart in her throat. *No*—not another victim. Taylor couldn't handle any more blood on her conscience. Wesley looked pale and scared, and there was a sheen of sweat on his forehead.

Neither of them wanted more people to die. Every time someone did, it was their failure.

Then Winchester said: "But this one's alive."

***

It was barely seven a.m. when Taylor knocked on Isabel Sweeney's door, the sun rising above the trees of Flyway City. The air was cool, and Taylor hugged herself. Wesley was behind her, standing a safe distance away. They hadn't talked about what happened between them, and Taylor was trying not to think about it. All that mattered right now was that the killer had struck again—but this victim, somehow, had gotten away.

Moments later, Isabel, a pretty young woman, answered the door. She had long, curly brown hair and eyes the color of a clear summer sky. Her home was warm and inviting, decorated with bright colors and fabrics. It smelled like lavender and vanilla, like a bakery on a warm day. But there was nothing warm on Isabel's face—in fact, she looked petrified.

"Are you the FBI agents I was told about?" she asked, her voice shaking.

Taylor held up her badge, and Wesley did the same. "I'm Special Agent Taylor Sage, and this is my partner, Special Agent John Wesley. Are you Isabel Sweeney?"

"Yes, that's me," Isabel said. "Please come in."

She led them through the house. It was small, but tastefully appointed. The decorating was mostly natural, with only a few odd touches here and there. There was a framed photograph on the wall of a waterfall, and a book and music player on the couch.

"Please have a seat," Isabel said, pointing to the couch. "Can I get you two anything?"

"No, thank you," Taylor said. "We're here to talk about what happened to you."

Isabel she sat down on the loveseat next to the couch. She folded her trembling hands in her lap and looked at them. Isabel's voice was shaking, and her eyes were filled with tears. Taylor's heart broke for her. She could tell that Isabel was completely confused, but she didn't know who to trust.

"It's okay," Taylor said. "Just start from the beginning."

"Okay." Isabel took a breath. "Well, I left my friend Fran's house around eleven last night. I knew about the warning not to go outside—I saw it on the news—but this neighborhood is so safe, I've walked around it a million times. My house is only a couple streets away from

Fran's, and I'd had some drinks, so I risked it. But then… I heard this… voice."

Taylor lifted an eyebrow. "What voice?"

"It sounded like a child saying 'help me.' But I thought I was hearing things. I mean, I'm partially deaf in my one ear, so… anyway, I kept walking, but then I saw this… thing."

Taylor exchanged a look with Wesley. This was getting weirder by the second.

"It was a doll," Isabel said. "A creepy little porcelain doll, just sitting in the middle of the sidewalk."

What the hell? Taylor couldn't help but frown as the image formed in her mind. That was… strange. Very strange. She kept quiet, listening as Isabel went on.

"Then I heard the voice again. But it was coming from behind me, so I spun around to see this guy standing there with a knife."

Taylor's pulse jumped. If she hadn't been convinced this was the same guy as before, she was now.

"What happened next?" Taylor asked.

"I just freaked out. I started running, and I didn't look back. I thought he was behind me the whole time. He yelled for me to stop, still in that voice."

Taylor could imagine it—the terror on Isabel's face, the sound of her footsteps pounding against the pavement. It was horrifying.

"Did you see his face?" Taylor asked.

Isabel shook her head. "No, but… I'm pretty sure it was the same guy who killed those other two women, because I've never seen anyone so scary around here."

"Right," Taylor said. "And the voice… you said it was coming from behind you. But the doll…" Suddenly, everything seemed to click into place for Taylor. "The voice you heard—he probably wanted you to think it was coming from the doll," she said slowly. "It was some kind of auditory trick, but it didn't work on you because of your hearing."

That must have been what this guy was luring women into alleys with.

First, the child's voice. He must have been doing that himself.

Then, the doll. The victim would probably be very confused as they approached.

And finally, the kill.

But it didn't work on Isabel—she'd been able to escape, and for that, Taylor was grateful. This information was huge. In fact, in changed everything.

This wasn't just the work of some killer randomly choosing women at night.

This was something more sinister, more twisted.

Isabel looked at her, and there was a glimmer of hope in her eyes. She knew she wasn't the only one who'd been attacked—but the FBI was on it now.

"Can you tell us what he looks like?" Taylor asked.

She shook her head again. "No, but… I think he might have been wearing a hood or something. He didn't look too old, but he could have been. I'm sorry, I really couldn't see his face."

Taylor and Wesley exchanged a look. This case was only getting more complex. What Taylor still didn't know was if the killer really was picking his victims at random, or if there was a connection. But having a *live* victim in front of her could change everything.

Taking out her phone, Taylor opened up a photo of Mary Gibbons. She showed it to Isabel. "Have you ever seen this woman before?"

Isabel looked at the photo, blinking. "No. Well, on the news, I did… She died, right?" Isabel shivered. "It's the same guy, isn't it? The one who attacked me—he killed her…"

Taylor nodded. "We are thinking that's the case." She flipped to a photo of Emily. "What about this woman? Do you know her?"

Once more, Isabel shook her head. "No, I've never seen her."

No luck. But Taylor had one more question to ask: "And have you ever been to any yoga or Pilates classes in town?"

"No, never," Isabel said. "Working out isn't really my thing…"

So, that was that, then. It seemed the Pilates connection had been a simple coincidence. Maybe the victims really were selected at random.

"Isabel," Taylor said finally, "we're going to do everything we can to find this guy. In the meantime, please stay inside after dark. We can send an officer to keep an eye on your house, since he was spotted around here. He might know where you live."

Isabel nodded, her face still pale but her eyes clear. She was starting to understand what they were saying—that she was not alone in this fight.

"Thank you," she said quietly. "I don't know what I'd do without you."

"Don't worry about it," Taylor said. "We'll get him."

Isabel stood up, and Taylor put her hand on her shoulder. "We're not stopping until we nail him, okay?"

Isabel smiled, but it felt forced.

Taylor knew it took a lot to overcome something like what Isabel had gone through, and she respected her for it.

With that, Taylor and Wesley left Isabel's house. They exchanged a look as they passed through the front door. This case was only getting more complex.

"So what do you think?" Taylor asked once they were outside.

Wesley sighed. "I don't know, but we've got to find out more about this guy. He's only killed two women so far, but he's definitely behind more attacks."

Taylor nodded. "Yes, I agree. In the meantime, we should leave Isabel alone. She's suffered enough already."

"I don't want her living in fear," Wesley said quietly. "Sometimes when we deal with cases like this, I can't help but think of my daughter, and it makes my blood burn knowing there are people out there who'd want to hurt her."

They approached the car. Taylor got in the passenger side while Wesley got behind the wheel. The car had a smell of coffee and leather. Taylor was getting used to being in its passenger seat.

"I agree," Taylor said. "Unfortunately, I think living in fear is the safest bet for the women in this town until we catch this guy."

This whole thing was terrifying, and it still made her heart race when she thought about it. But that was why they were doing their best to catch him before he could hurt any other women.

Taylor took out her phone and called the local PD, telling them to send an officer to keep an eye on Isabel's house until further notice. As she hung up, Wesley began driving through the city.

Taylor ruminated on the case. This one had seemed like a pretty standard psycho killing women in alleyways, but this new information added an entirely new layer to the crime. The doll, the child's voice… it all had to mean something. Taylor just wasn't sure what yet.

Taylor had worked some seriously disturbing cases in her career, and she had a gut feeling this one was about to get weirder.

CHAPTER FIFTEEN

Back at the hotel room, Taylor sat across from Wesley with her laptop out, trying not to think about how just a few hours ago, she'd been on that bed with him, trapped in his arms. Instead, she focused on the screen in front of her as she typed out what she thought might become a good profile for the killer.

"Okay, so," Taylor said. "We know he has a porcelain doll."

"Right," Wesley said. "Which is beyond creepy, might I add."

"I know." Taylor nodded. "But it could be significant. His attachment to the doll could definitely tell us something about who he is. It could tell us that he's still attached to his childhood."

Wesley nodded. "I think you're right. The doll could be a key piece of information in this case."

"It's possible," Taylor said, typing away on her laptop. "In fact, I think it's something we should focus on."

She glanced up at Wesley and saw the interest in his eyes. "What do you think?"

"I agree," Wesley said immediately. "If we can find out what the doll means to the killer, we might be able to find out more about his motives."

Taylor nodded and resumed typing, thinking hard about what they could do next. It was definitely an interesting angle to explore, and she was optimistic that they would find something useful in regards to the doll.

But there was something else about Isabel's report that stood out to Taylor. And that was the "child's voice."

Surely, the man they were after wasn't a child at all. He must have been doing some sort of vocal trick, something to make it sound like he was young. He'd lure the girls in with the voice, make them think a child was in danger, then they'd see the doll and become confused… and then he'd strike.

Taylor shivered just thinking about the type of man who would do something like this.

"To bend his voice like that," Taylor said, "maybe he's a voice actor or something like that."

"Yeah, it's crazy the way some people can alter their voices," Wesley said. "I hear it all the time on Maisie's cartoons when she's watching them at home. Most of the voice actors on TV are grown adults. They just have a weird talent."

Taylor nodded. "Maybe the killer has it too."

She thought back to the doll, and the creepy image she had of it in her head. Maybe it was too simplistic to think it was just a voice actor. Taylor couldn't just think about each clue individually; she had to think about them together. How they worked together.

"What if," she said, "the doll and the voice are connected?"

"How do you mean?" Wesley asked.

"I mean… maybe the killer isn't just some voice actor. Maybe he's a ventriloquist."

"A ventriloquist?" Wesley leaned back in his chair and crossed his arms.

"Yes," Taylor said. "Maybe he uses the doll in his act, then uses it to do the voice on the other women."

"Possible," Wesley said. "So we should look into ventriloquists in town. I doubt there's many of them; it's sort of a dying art."

"Exactly," Taylor said, and she turned back to her laptop, opening her internet browser. She had that gut feeling again—the feeling that told her she was onto something. She was getting closer… she just needed to find all the right pieces, and put them together in the right order.

As Taylor went to search online, her phone rang and pulled her back to reality. She'd gotten lost in the case and had swept away her nightmare about Angie. And the fact that she still hadn't heard from the hospital.

Her heart leapt as she checked her phone. But it wasn't the hospital.

It was her father.

"Dad," she said, a little surprised to hear from him at all.

"Taylor," her father said, "I just wanted to check up on you. Are you alright?"

"I'm fine," Taylor said. "I'm working a case."

A heavy pause hung between them. Across the table, Wesley focused on his laptop as Taylor spoke.

"What's going on, Dad?" Taylor asked, but after last night's nightmare, she was a little afraid of the answers. "Has Angie woken up again?"

Her dad sighed. "No, sweetheart. She hasn't."

"Oh," Taylor said. Her stomach lurched, and she felt a mixture of relief and fear.

"One of the nurses came to talk to me," her father continued. "She said that when Angie woke up, before they sedated her, she seemed… confused. We're a little worried about who she might be when she wakes up for real."

Taylor's stomach clenched. This was a reality she didn't want to face. "Dad, Angie will be okay," she said. "I'm sure she's been waiting for us to save her all these years."

"I hope so," her father said. "But we both know this isn't something we can predict."

"Maybe." Taylor nodded. "But Angie's strong."

"You're right," her father said. "And I know you are strong too."

"Thank you," Taylor said, and felt tears in the back of her eyes. She felt so grateful for her dad.

"I've got to go now," her father said. "But I'll be back to see you as soon as I know what's going on."

"Okay, Dad," Taylor said. "I love you."

"I love you too," her father said.

The call ended, and Taylor sat in silence for a moment. Her head began to pound. Maybe she hadn't slept enough, after all.

Wesley eyed her from across the table. "You okay?" he asked.

Taylor nodded. "Thanks, Wes. For being here."

"Of course." He gave her a half smile, then went back to his research. "Well, I've got a bit of good news. While you were on the phone, I found this guy."

He turned the screen to Taylor, and she was met with an image of a cartoonish-looking man with a curly mustache. Next to him was a ventriloquist doll. The name on the article read "Willie Vanderwolf."

"He was really popular," Wesley said, "until he lost his job as a performer."

"What'd he do?" Taylor asked. This Willie guy definitely looked creepy enough.

"Here." Wesley took his laptop back, clicked a few times, then slid it back over to Taylor.

On the screen was an article called BELOVED VENTRILOQUIST EXPOSED AS FRAUD!

Taylor scanned the article, absorbing all of the information. Willie was accused of using a voice-altering device to pull off his different voices for his characters. He'd allegedly use the same device to produce his voice, so that he could appear to his audiences to be a childlike figure.

The article also said that Willie and the ventriloquist doll had been a hit in a touring show until something went wrong at a performance. The show had been booked at the Royal Variety Show, which was held in front of a large crowd.

According to the article, Willie had performed the act, then suddenly the ventriloquist doll's mouth moved and produced a voice. Willie tried to cover it up, and people seemed to believe him and move on.

Until one person decided to expose him for good.

Her name was Kat Delaney. Apparently, Delaney had recorded evidence of Willie faking his stunts and reported him. He'd lost his job, had his reputation ruined. Everything went downhill for him from there.

There was a photo of Kat Delaney in the article.

Taylor's stomach dropped.

Kat happened to be a pretty young woman—just like the killer's victims.

Mind whirring, Taylor leaned back. Maybe Willie had started targeting random women in the night as a power play to get back at Kat, who would be too difficult for him to kill in real life. It'd be too traceable, Taylor figured. But Willie could kill random women in the night and get away with it. He could lure them out with his voice, then grab them with his right hand, slit their throat with his left.

She looked up a video of Willie performing. It took place on a stage, and Taylor clicked play. The video started moving. It showed Willie, with his left hand holding a ventriloquist doll. And then, the voice… it made Taylor's skin crawl. She clicked away from the video and exchanged a look with Wesley, who was watching beside her.

"I think we need to pay this guy a visit," Taylor said.

CHAPTER SIXTEEN

It wasn't fair. He'd done everything right. In the dark kitchen, he got down on his knees as Betty sat on the chair, looking down at him with her glassy, disapproving eyes.

"I did it all, just like you said," he whimpered. He hated the sound of his own voice. But he hated himself more. He'd let her down. "I put you out for her to see, I used my voice to catch her attention, but…"

Despair slammed into his chest. Tears poured from his eyes, rolled down his cheeks, and splashed onto the tile floor.

"I did everything you said, Betty, but it wasn't good enough. She… she blindsided me! She got away!"

Not good enough, Betty said inside his mind. He looked up at her, stared at her eyes and black-painted lips. Her mouth didn't move when she spoke, but he knew she was communicating with him. They had a special connection.

He hated letting her down more than anything in the world.

You need to find another, Betty commanded. *A different one. A better one.*

"I will," he said. "Betty, I will." He scrambled up to the chair, still on his knees, and looked up at her. He was her subject, and she was his ruler. "Tell me who," he said. "Just say who and I'll make sure I get it right. Do you want another girl?"

Betty didn't answer.

She just sat there with her arms crossed, looking down at him.

"What is it, Betty?" he said. "What did I do wrong?"

Uh-uh, Betty said. *No more girls. Bad enough you were out for wrong girl. Now you want me to point you toward another wrong one?*

"But I did everything you said!" he argued. "I was so careful! I bent over backwards to follow every detail. You said I'd make a perfect subject, and now you're telling me that I'm a failure? That I couldn't find another one to replace her?"

I don't know what happened, she said. *You need to do better.*

He'd worked so hard to please her, to give her the power that she craved. He'd paid attention to her every word, obeyed her every command, and done exactly what she said, even when he didn't understand or didn't like it. But that hadn't been enough.

"Tell me how to fix this," he pleaded.

But Betty didn't respond. He hated it when she shut him out—it hurt more than anything in the whole world. It hurt more than when his father would beat him. Nothing hurt him more than letting Betty town.

He let out a painful grunt. He knew what she wanted from him now. He'd have to figure it out on his own.

The girls hadn't been enough to please her so far, but what if… what if…

A smile curled at his lips. "Betty. I've figured it out." He slowly rose to his feet and picked her up, hugging her tight. "Don't worry. I know what to do now. The girls weren't good enough…"

He set her down and smiled, bright and toothy.

"So how about a boy?"

CHAPTER SEVENTEEN

Taylor crept up to the house that Willie Vanderwolf lived in. Apparently, his years as a professional ventriloquist had paid off, and he had been able to afford a nice home. The house was made of brick and had a large front porch with a big, ornate door. There were two large windows on either side of the door, and the porch was surrounded by a large, ivy-covered fence.

There was a car in the driveway.

Looking over her shoulder, Taylor locked eyes with Wesley, who nodded. Willie was home.

They didn't know for sure if Vanderwolf was their guy—but he was definitely worth checking out. The fact that the woman who exposed him was a pretty young woman, just like the victims, made Taylor pause. And he was a ventriloquist, too; he probably had a vendetta against the world for shutting him out. But as of right now, it was just a theory, and Taylor needed proof.

The window was slightly ajar, and Taylor could see Vanderwolf inside. His hair was mussed and he was rubbing his eyes, as if he had just woken up. He was wearing a white T-shirt and blue jeans, and he looked tired. There was a look of confusion on his face, as if he didn't understand why he was there. He was holding a coffee cup, and the smell of coffee filled the air, creeping out through the window.

But wait…

Taylor squinted. He was talking to someone.

There was someone else there.

A woman came into view. But it wasn't just any woman.

That brown hair, those brown eyes…

It was Kat Delaney. The woman who'd exposed him.

Taylor's heart began to pound. Kat was here, in Willie's house. They were enemies. What if…

Taylor shot Wesley a look and whispered, "Wes, it's Kat Delaney. He has her."

Wesley crept over and peered into the window. "Damn. We need to get in there. What if he's—"

"My thoughts exactly."

They took their guns out and went up to the door. Taylor feared the worst—that Willie really was the killer, and now he had Kat, and was ready to take her out too.

But as they got closer, they could see that there was no way in. The door was locked.

They heard Vanderwolf say something. Taylor peered through another window. Then Kat went over to him and hugged him. He looked surprised, but he didn't push her away. They hugged for a few seconds, and then she pulled away, looking embarrassed.

"I'm sorry, Willie," she said. "It's all my fault."

She started to walk away, but Vanderwolf called her back.

"Kat," he said softly. "Please...stay with me."

Kat hesitated for a moment, and then she went back to him. They stood there together, holding each other. Taylor shot Wesley a confused look. Based on that conversation...

It didn't sound like they were enemies at all.

Just as Taylor was about to call this whole thing off, the door swung open, and Kat came rushing out—but Willie was chasing after her.

"Kat, wait!"

That was when he noticed Taylor and Wesley.

Willie Vanderwolf looked different in person. He had a large, graying beard and a grandfatherly face. He was much less theatrical than he had looked online. Kat noticed Taylor and Wesley too and screamed, seeing their guns.

Taylor quickly put hers away.

"We're with the FBI," she said, showing her badge. "We need to ask you a couple of questions."

Vanderwolf sighed. "I already have to answer so many questions," he said. "But I guess it's okay. Who am I going to tell next?"

"Willie, what's going on?" Kat asked.

"They're probably here about that damn article, Kat..."

Taylor frowned. "Like I said, we're with the FBI. The article isn't why we're here."

"But you know about it," Willie said.

Taylor wasn't getting killer vibes from Willie at all—but still, she was here, and looks could be deceiving. Maybe he wanted to kill Kat, but couldn't, so he went after the other women...?

"You're Kat Delaney, right?" Taylor asked. "The one mentioned in the article exposing Willie?"

"Yes," Kat said, looking guilty. "But… things were different then. Willie is trying. That's why I'm here."

"What do you mean?" Wesley asked, squaring up.

"She's teaching me how to be a real ventriloquist," Willie explained.

"It looked like you were doing more than that," Wesley commented.

Kat and Willie exchanged a look. "It got… complicated," Willie said.

Complicated was right. This wasn't what Taylor was expecting when she came here.

"Well," she said, "I'd still like to ask you a few questions. Both of you."

"Of course," Willie said. "If it's for the FBI…" He gestured for them to enter.

Taylor stepped inside, and Wesley followed. Vanderwolf's house was large, with a living room and dining room, both decorated with the same, eclectic taste of old prints and paintings. Both were filled with sofas and chairs, tables and lamps, and old, dusty books halfway to the ceiling.

Vanderwolf gestured for them to sit on a regal couch, so they did. There was a funny-looking grandfather clock, but as soon as Taylor looked at it, the hands jumped forward, and she wondered if it was in time with the rest of the house.

The living room was decorated with a lot of old vases, but each was made of different kinds of ceramic. Kat and Willie awkwardly sat down on the other couch.

"Look," Kat said, "whatever this is about, our relationship… it's a secret, okay?"

Taylor looked at her, then at Willie. "Mr. Vanderwolf. Ms. Delaney… we're looking into the recent murders in town."

"Murders?" Vanderwolf said, his eyes widening. "What do you mean, murders?"

Taylor and Wesley exchanged a look.

"You haven't heard?" Taylor asked.

"I've been very focused on trying to get back into work," Willie said.

But Kat—her face was pale. "I heard," she said quietly. "You mean the women who were killed in the alleyways."

Taylor and Wesley nodded.

"We were told not to go out after dark," Kat said.

"That's right," Taylor said. She paused, figuring she might as well not beat around the bush. "Mr. Vanderwolf, we came here today because we're looking for someone who is altering their voice. I can't say much more than that, but we do think there could be a connection between that 'talent' and the recent crimes."

Willie went pale, the realization seeming to dawn over him. "Wait—you think I'm a suspect?"

Taylor was quiet.

"It's not possible," Kat said. She glanced at Willie. "He, well, he isn't making any progress. Willie cannot alter his voice at all without digital assistance. We're working on it, but…"

Willie looked at his lap. "I never was as good as I said I was."

"No, you were never as good as you said you were," Kat said quietly. Willie looked at her in shame. "But you're learning, and you're changing. And that's more than enough. There's a lot of good in people."

"You don't understand," Willie said. "I wanted to be good on my own."

"Yes, you did," Kat said. "It's true you were never able to complete a trick. But you were trying."

"I was…not good enough."

"But I'm doing everything I can to help you."

As touching as the moment was, if Willie wasn't their guy, then Taylor needed to move on. Maybe this trip didn't need to be a total waste of time.

"Willie," Taylor began. "You've been involved in the world of ventriloquism for a long time. Can you think of anyone else who might be helpful to us in the investigation?"

"No." Vanderwolf shook his head. "I don't know who would want to hurt the women in town."

"Someone who's angry," Wesley said. "Or someone with a vendetta."

Vanderwolf thought for a moment, then rubbed at the back of his neck. "Well… actually…" He looked at Kat, as if for reassurance. "There is this one guy."

"You mean…?" Kat asked, and Willie nodded.

They both looked at the agents. Taylor leaned forward, eager to hear what he had to say.

"Marty Phillips," Willie said.

"He's huge right now," Kat added. "A major ventriloquist who does huge shows across the state. And his voice work—it's real. I've met him myself."

Willie shifted his weight, uncomfortable. "He's sort of… taken up the disgraced spotlight I left behind."

"But here's the thing," Kat said. "Marty isn't such a great guy. He's been accused of sexually harassing girls. He gave me creepy vibes as well, although he never said anything to me upfront."

"He's a respected figure," Willie said. "He used to be on the fringes, but he's been pulling in a lot of attention with his shows."

"But if he's got a reputation for sexually harassing, then why are people so willing to work for him?" Taylor asked.

"He's famous," Kat explained. "He's famous, and he's a big name. People sign up to work for him because they think he's a good guy, and they want to help him out. You know how it is with powerful men in any industry. They get away with things for too long…" Kat shot Willie a look, and he looked away in shame.

After all this, Taylor was feeling confident that Willie Vanderwolf was a dead end. But this Marty Phillips guy—this could lead somewhere. A local man who could alter his voice, and also had a criminal history, sounded much more promising.

"But last I heard," Kat added, "Marty's on tour right now, so I don't know if he's in town."

Damn. Taylor would have to figure out where he was—and she hoped it wouldn't be far.

Taylor stood up, and Wesley followed. "Thanks for your time," Taylor said. "We'll be in touch if anything comes up."

Willie and Kat stood too. "I'm sorry if we weren't more help," Kat said.

"You were," Taylor said. "We'll look into Marty Phillips. Thank you."

With that, Taylor and Wesley left the odd couple, into the cool morning. Taylor sighed as Willie's door closed behind them. She took out her phone and called HQ, directing herself to June Willoughby, a tech who'd helped her on the Gabe French case.

"Hi, June," Taylor said as she walked toward Wesley's car, parked on the street in the morning light.

"Special Agent Sage!" June exclaimed. "So great to hear from you! How can I help?"

Across from Taylor, Wesley got in the driver's side, and Taylor got in the other side. She shut the door and settled into the seat.

"June, I'm looking into a ventriloquist over here in Flyway City. His name's Marty Phillips. I need to know where he is; lead mentioned he might be on tour."

"Give me a sec..." Through the phone, Taylor could hear a keyboard clacking.

"Okay, here's the information you're looking for. Marty Phillips is currently in Ashland—that's about an hour away from Flyway."

A sense of adrenaline coursed through Taylor. That wasn't far. "Do you have any other info on him?"

"A bit," June said. "He's been accused of sexual harassment in the past, but he's been getting a lot of good press lately because of his successful shows. He's also got a criminal record—assault, trespassing... things like that."

"That sounds like someone I want to talk to," Taylor said. "Anything else?"

"Well, the guy has a surprisingly big social media following for his line of work," June said.

Taylor paused, considering this. Willie didn't have a social media presence. But Taylor considered, for a moment, that the victims weren't chosen at random. If Marty had access to copious numbers of strangers online, maybe that was how he'd decided who to pick. June was an expert on digging up people's dirt, so Taylor decided to throw one more thing at her, to see if there was any connection between Marty and any of the victims.

"It might be a shot in the dark, but I have two victims—Emily Johnson and Mary Gibbons. Can you find any connection between them and Marty? Maybe a social media connection? Both girls are from Flyway City."

June clacked away, until she said: "A woman named Mary Gibbons follows one of Marty's profiles."

Taylor's mouth went dry. "And the other?"

"No, ma'am. Just the one."

Taylor nodded. "Thank you, June. You've been a big help. Send me the address I need to go to, okay?"

"On it! Good luck, Special Agent Sage."

With that, they hung up. But Taylor wasn't sure what to make of it. So Mary had followed Marty online. But Emily didn't. Maybe it didn't mean anything, but it was still a connection between one of the victims and the suspect. They needed to run this down.

Taylor pulled her seatbelt on and looked at Wesley, who was avoiding eye contact.

"June's sending me an address, but start toward Ashland. Marty's doing a show there. Mary followed him on social media."

Wesley silently nodded and started the car, and Taylor couldn't help but notice that he was being unusually quiet.

"You okay?" she tried to ask.

Wesley was quiet, unable to look at her.

Taylor's heart dropped. "Wesley, what's wrong?"

"It's just…" He shook his head. His eyes were focused on the road as he navigated through the town, but Taylor couldn't help but feel anxious. "I was thinking about those two, and their 'secret relationship'…"

Taylor's throat tightened. "What about it?"

"I feel like I got too touchy with you earlier. I'm sorry for that. Really."

Taylor's heart softened at the apology. Wesley was definitely a complex guy, with a lot of hidden emotions. But she trusted him, and she knew he would always have her back.

"It's okay," Taylor said, trying to reassure him. "I… wasn't upset about it."

She didn't know what else to say. The whole situation was strange, and she wasn't sure what Wesley was feeling. But as long as he was okay… that was all that mattered.

But Wesley kept looking guilty. He was probably thinking that they should keep things professional. And the rational part of Taylor knew that too, even though the thought gave her heart a strange, foreign ache.

"We should… keep things professional," Taylor said, looking away.

"Yeah," Wesley said. "It's probably better that way."

But for whatever reason, this conversation was making Taylor's chest hurt. She had not been with anyone since Ben, and being in Wesley's arms earlier made her feel so… safe.

But it was wrong. Knew that. They were partners. For a moment, she told herself that maybe Belasco's warning *was* about Wesley breaking her heart. If she focused on that, it would be easier to forget her… other feelings.

It had to end there.

But still. In her heart, Taylor didn't believe that he would hurt her. She focused forward, watching the world pass by as they drove to Ashland in silence.

CHAPTER EIGHTEEN

Taylor unbuckled her seatbelt as Wesley parked the car. Ashland wasn't exactly a bustling city, but it had a few nice parts. The building where Marty Phillips was performing was an old opera house, still in good condition. The parking lot was clogged with cars and vans, and the people who were milling about outside were of all ages. They weren't all there for him—there was a carnival going on in the parking lot. Various rides stretched into the mid-morning sky.

"Think he's in there?" Wesley asked, still in the driver's seat.

"I hope so," Taylor said. "He's supposed to be preparing for an afternoon performance linked to the carnival, so… he should be getting ready."

Wesley nodded. "Let's go."

They got out of the car and made their way across the parking lot, gaining a few curious looks from pedestrians. Taylor knew their overly black outfits made them look like stiffs—not exactly the types to be at a carnival or ventriloquist show.

As they entered the opera house, Taylor was surprised at the size. It had a spacious lobby, decorated with gilded mirrors and ornate furniture. Their shoes clacked against the tile as they went through a pair of double doors that led to the auditorium. It was decorated with beautiful stained glass windows and plush red velvet seats. The stage was brightly lit, but the room was empty.

"Hey!" someone said.

Taylor looked around. There was a man with clownish makeup on his cheeks and chin, a bell-shaped nose on his face, and a red wig. He was wearing a flowery-print shirt and an eye-patch.

"I'm Jet Wannabe, the ventriloquist's assistant," he said, extending his hand.

"Taylor Sage, FBI," she said.

Surprise crossed his jovial face. "Oh, the FBI? Is this a silly trick?"

"Not at all," Wesley said, his voice hard. "We're looking for Marty Phillips."

"Oh, my! What has Marty done this time?"

"This time?" Taylor asked.

Jet shied away. "Well… I shouldn't say…"

"Where is he?" Taylor asked. She didn't have time for whatever performance this person was putting on.

Was this a joke? Did Marty really need some clown to be his assistant?

"Marty's offstage." Jet pointed them toward the back of the stage. "He's in the green room—this way."

As they navigated a labyrinth of rooms and hallways in search of Marty Phillips, Taylor felt like she was in a claustrophobic horror movie. Jet was darting around them, keeping up a constant stream of colorful banter. Taylor could probably have found Marty Phillips herself, but she appreciated the man's enthusiasm.

"Where's Marty?" she asked.

"Right here!" Jet said, ducking into a room.

Taylor waited a moment, and then walked inside. The room was mostly bare, with only a chair and a few boxes on the floor. A mirror hung on the wall, and a small lightbulb hung above them. A mound of unidentifiable objects was piled in the corner.

"What is that?" Taylor asked, pointing at the pile.

Jet tittered nervously. "Oh, that's Marty's… you know."

Taylor glared at him. He needed to give them some sort of hint as to what that was.

"He—he makes costumes for the show," Jet said finally. "You know, masks and things."

"So he's not here?" Wesley asked.

"N-no," Jet said, his face turning red. "I thought he might be—but he isn't."

Wesley shot Taylor an irritated look. Taylor nodded, showing him that she was thinking the same thing.

Was this Jet person wasting their time?

Taylor immediately turned and left the room, Wesley behind her. Jet chased after them. "Wait, wait!"

But Taylor ignored him. Maybe he was buying Marty time, she didn't know, but she stormed into the auditorium and headed for the stage. She made it just as Jet stepped into the ring of light that illuminated the backstage area. She almost walked straight past him.

"Wait!" he said, holding out his arms.

"What is this?" she asked. "You're not with Marty… and you know what he did?"

"I can't say," Jet said.

"If you're wasting our time," Wesley said, "then I'm going to have to arrest you."

Jet looked back at Taylor, and then at Wesley. His face turned white, but he stood his ground. "I had to see you here," he said. "I don't know what Marty's done, but I know there's something wrong."

"Then tell us," Taylor said.

"I can't, I can't—" Jet said. "I'm not allowed to. It's just not done."

"What?" Wesley asked.

"I know it's crazy… I know it's—" Jet was stuttering like crazy. "I'm not allowed to know. Everyone knows, everyone knows. It's not allowed. It's the rules. I'm not allowed to say, I'm not allowed to know."

Wesley was staring at him in disbelief. "So… you know. And you're not allowed to say anything."

"Yeah!" Jet said, nodding. "Yeah!"

"What is this?" Taylor asked. This guy was making no sense. "Jet, I'm going to have to ask you to step aside; you're interfering with a federal investigation, and that in itself is a crime."

Jet stared at them, his eyes wide with fear. He seemed to be twitching like crazy, like he was having a seizure. His mouth was wide open, his eyes wild.

"Jet, I'm going to have to ask you to step aside," she said, more firmly this time.

This time, he did.

Taylor and Wesley shoved past him and went backstage. They ripped past a curtain that separated the stage from a mock dressing room—and that was when they saw him.

Marty Phillips.

Jet scrambled up behind them. "Marty, they're FBI!"

Marty's face went pale—before he booked it. He turned and bolted through the curtain.

Taylor and Wesley chased after him. He was fast, but Taylor caught up with him just in time.

She held up her badge. "FBI! Freeze!"

But as Taylor was chasing Marty, she noticed something odd. He was on his phone as he ran, as if trying to delete things from it.

Marty flung open the door to a storage room and darted through it. Taylor and Wesley smashed into the room together after him. The door slammed shut, and they were plunged into darkness. The room smelled of old, musty clothes and dirty feet. There were boxes stacked up to the ceiling, and a large, rusty water tank sat in the center of the room. The room was small, and it was crammed full of boxes and old furniture. The only light came from a single, dirty window, and it was barely enough to see by.

“Marty Phillips,” Taylor called out cautiously. They didn’t have full vision, so she had to be careful. “We’re just here to talk, Marty,” Taylor said. She could barely see him, but she felt Wesley’s heat near her, reminding her that she had backup.

“Wha—what are you doing here?” Marty asked, his voice breaking. It sounded like it could have been coming from anywhere in the room.

“We’re here to talk, Marty,” Wesley said, his voice hard. “You need to talk. Right now, Marty. I want to know everything.”

“Nothing’s happened,” Marty said. “I didn’t do anything.”

“What were you removing from your phone, Marty?” Taylor asked.

“Nothing!” Marty said, his voice even more panicked. “I—I don’t know what you think I did, but I didn’t do anything like that.”

“I saw you, Marty,” Taylor said, still creeping through the room. “Why don’t you come out and talk to us about what happened?”

Marty stuttered away from them. “You saw me—what? Did I do something?”

Wesley caught up with Taylor. “Where are you, Marty?”

“I—I’m hiding out,” Marty said. He sounded like he was crying. “I’m not going to talk, I’m not going to talk. I’m not going to talk!”

“I won’t ask you again,” Wesley said. “You need to come out. Now.”

There was a long silence. Then, suddenly, the door to the room opened, letting a sliver of light in. Taylor whirred around.

Marty slipped out through the door, back into the hallway.

“Son of a bitch!” Taylor yelled.

They didn’t think twice—they just went after him.

Taylor and Wesley chased after Marty, their footsteps echoing through the hallway. They turned another corner, and there he was—running away down another hall.

“Halt!” Taylor called out.

Marty didn’t stop, didn’t even turn around. He kept running until he reached the other end of the hall, where he stopped to catch his breath. He was panting hard, his eyes wide with fear.

“Marty,” Taylor said. “That’s enough. Give it up.”

Marty didn’t move. He just stood there.

"Marty," Taylor said again. "It's over. Come out now and we can talk."

Her voice was hard, but she could see the wavering in Marty's eyes. He was terrified, and he didn't seem to have much control over himself.

"Please," he whispered. "Just let me go."

"I can't do that," Taylor said. "You need to come down to the station with us."

She started to approach him, but then there was a loud noise from down the hall. They both turned to look as a group of people—several men and women—walked into the hallway, their shocked expressions clear on their faces.

"What is going on here?" one of the men asked, stepping forward unsteadily. He was tall and wearing a suit, and looked like he was in charge. "Who are you?"

Taylor flashed her badge. "We're with the FBI. This man is coming with us."

In the back, a camera flashed as Taylor grabbed Marty and slapped cuffs on him.

It was over for him—and the whole world would know it.

CHAPTER NINETEEN

It was too bright out for him to work. But he didn't have a choice. Betty would be disappointed if he didn't finish what he'd started. He had to go back there—to that street where he'd once lived with his father. It had to be there. Betty wouldn't have it any other way.

He walked down the suburb street under the cerulean daytime sky. He waved at an elderly woman watering her plants. He nodded at a man walking his dog. The street was long and narrow street lined with neat, white houses. There were children playing in the yards and a cat sunning itself on the porch. The houses were spaced far apart, and the street was quiet except for the sound of the water and the rustling of the leaves

It was all too public.

Betty was tucked in his bag. "Betty," he whispered to her, "how can I pull this off? Someone will see..."

Figure out it, she said back. *If you don't—*

"I'll get beat again," he said. "I know. I won't let you down."

And he wouldn't. Betty deserved happiness. He would give it to her. He just needed to find a way...

Up ahead was the spot where he'd lost the last girl. The one who'd run away. No one had ever escaped him before, and his blood burned just thinking about it.

He had to try. He could lose himself in the suburb if he had to. It no longer mattered. He could lose himself and never come back. He'd do anything just to keep Betty safe. He shook his head. Then he'd be no better than his father. He'd fallen into the same trap his father had. He would not let that happen to Betty.

He walked up to the house he'd been in before. It was different now. The house was nothing but concrete blocks, but the street was still lined with neat white houses. The lawns were overgrown. There was a pile of garbage in the driveway. He squinted through the glass. No one was home. He went to the back and saw the fence for the first time. He hadn't noticed it before. It was too low. He hopped over it.

He walked down the well-kept lawn to the rear of the house. He had so many memories here. Whoever lived here now was clearly not home. They didn't appreciate it the same way he did. They didn't go through what he did here.

"Is this good, Betty?" he asked. "Would here do?"

Here is fine... here will do.

Good. He had an idea.

He crept along the side of the house, opening the fence so he could easily pass through. He placed Betty at the side of the house and smoothed out her dress, patting down her hair.

"I'll make this right," he vowed.

Then he went to the back of the house and waited. He peered around the corner. A few people passed, none of them good enough. He needed a lull in the traffic. He needed just one person... one man.

In the distance, he saw someone walking along the street. He stood up. The man was young, and he looked innocent enough. That was fine; he was alone, and no one else was around, so he would do wonderfully. He would make Betty happy.

He knew what had to be done.

He took a deep breath. He hated using his voice. But for Betty, he had to.

"Help... me..." he spoke out. He sounded like a child. It made even him sick. Every time he opened his mouth, he heard his father's voice again, felt his father's belt on his backside.

But using his voice worked. Betty commanded it. And so, he did it.

The man walking on the street paused and glanced over.

"Help... me..."

He was hidden behind the wall, so he didn't know for sure if his target had heard. He shut his eyes and listened for footsteps. There were none.

"Help... me..." he tried again.

Then he heard it: the footsteps coming close.

"Hello?" his target called out. "Is somebody there?"

"This way," he said. "Help me, please..."

The footsteps drew closer. His target should have seen Betty by now.

He took a deep breath and drew his knife.

It was time. He had to act fast.

He peered around the corner, where his target was looking down at Betty in confusion.

He pulled his hood up and held the knife at the ready.

Now was his time to strike.

For you, Betty, I'll make it all right.

CHAPTER TWENTY

Taylor sat in the Flyway Precinct with Wesley, going through all the evidence on Marty Phillips's phone. She flicked through the messages he was trying to delete, while Wesley looked over her shoulder.

"Jesus," Wesley said. "This guy's a piece of work."

Taylor couldn't agree more. Marty's phone was full of lewd messages and threats to women. Every time Taylor looked at them, she felt sick to her stomach. The evidence was overwhelming. It was clear that Marty was a danger to women, and he needed to be stopped.

But nothing in his phone pointed to him being responsible for the deaths of Emily Johnson or Mary Gibbons.

In fact, Taylor could see from his photo history that on the night Mary died, he was in another town, taking a photo of himself from a hotel balcony. It was timestamped and everything. If anything, this was solid evidence that Marty wasn't the killer.

No, this wasn't looking good for Marty's guilt. But Taylor wanted to interrogate him anyway—he'd still run away, and he was still a ventriloquist. He was waiting in the next room over, handcuffed.

"Should we go in?" Taylor asked, standing up.

Wesley got up and nodded. "Might as well. The guy still ran from us, and he's clearly guilty of harassment, at the very least."

"That's a good point," Taylor said, as she and Wesley headed out and entered the interrogation room. The room was small, with a metal table and chairs, and a single window that was covered by a metal grate. A single light bulb hung from the ceiling. It cast a yellow light over the room, making everything look dingy. Taylor took a deep breath. She could feel the tight knot in her stomach.

Marty was glaring at them from across the table. "I knew you were cops," he said.

"We're not cops," Taylor replied, sitting down with Wesley beside her. "We're with the FBI."

"Same thing, different story," Marty said. "I didn't do anything to anyone, so you have no reason to keep me here. Let me go."

"You were quite adamant about deleting those messages from your phone," Taylor said, ignoring him. "We were able to recover them anyway. You've been harassing a lot of women, Marty."

Marty shifted in his seat. "Yeah, but you know what? Those weren't real women. They were just fakes. They normally don't even reply."

"We're not interested in your 'fake' women," Wesley said, taking a step forward. "You've been attacking them verbally, threatening them. That's not something we can ignore."

"I never hurt anyone," Marty said.

"Where were you two nights ago, Marty?" Taylor asked, although she'd seen the evidence in his phone that he wasn't in Flyway City. Still… she wanted to hear it from him. More than anything, she wanted Marty to be the killer so she could stop him, then go and check on Angie.

"Oh, please," Marty said. "I was literally in a hotel all night three towns over from here. My manager had security keeping me in my room and everything because they didn't want me getting drunk and being photographed. So I was in my room all night, on my phone, talking to girls. Talking to them. Not harassing them. They like it when I talk to them, okay?"

Damn, Taylor thought. It was all lining up in Marty's favor. They'd confirm it with the manager, but so far, Marty Phillips was not looking like the killer. Just a regular douchebag with an affinity for sending unsolicited pictures and messages to women.

Either way, Taylor pulled up a photo of Mary on her phone and showed it to Marty. "Do you recognize this woman?"

He looked at her, then just shrugged. "No?"

"She follows you on social media," Taylor said.

"So? Lots of people do. I don't know her."

Taylor sighed. Even with the flimsy connection, she had nothing on Marty. It was another dead end. The real killer was still on the loose, and he was still walking around, still killing.

Marty growled. "I have nothing to do with whatever you're accusing me of. I have nothing to do with any of this. You don't have a case against me. I'm innocent. I've told you that a hundred times. If you're going to keep me here, then I'm going to lose my job and my career. I told you I haven't done anything."

Taylor sighed and looked at Marty Phillips. He was sitting there in his blue hoodie, staring at her with a look in his eye that told her he wasn't going to give her anything more than they already had.

"All right," she said, standing up. "We'll send an officer in to deal with you and the messages you've been sending women. If anything else comes up, we'll be in touch."

"Wait, that's it?" Marty asked. "Don't I get an explanation? I'm gonna sue you for this, you know!"

"Go right ahead," Wesley muttered, standing and following Taylor as she went for the exit. Marty kept yelling after them.

Once in the hallway, Taylor sighed and faced Wesley. "He's not our guy."

"Clearly not," Wesley said. "So, what now?"

Taylor didn't know. She'd really felt like she was onto something with the ventriloquist angle, but maybe she wasn't looking in the right place.

She took a breath and checked her phone.

There was a missed call from her dad.

Taylor's heart jumped. "Wes," she said, "I have to make a call."

Taylor took a deep breath and tried to control the shaking in her hands. She paced down the hallway in the station where she could be alone and called her dad. Her dad always made her feel better, even when she was really upset. She knew he could hear her in his mind, so she just spoke straight to him.

She was relieved when her dad picked up on the first ring. "Hey, Taylor," he said. "How are you doing?"

"I'm okay," Taylor lied. She couldn't really say anything else without going into too much detail, and she didn't want to do that over the phone. "I saw you called?"

"Right…" Her dad took a breath. "Taylor. Angie woke up. But she's… not doing well."

Taylor's heart sank like a stone in the ocean. "What do you mean?"

"Taylor, she… she didn't seem to recognize me."

"What do you mean?"

"I don't know. She just… didn't know who I was. I went and got her a glass of water, and she just stared at me. Not with a look of recognition, but something else. I don't know. She's not doing well, Taylor. She wasn't reacting to anything."

"I'm not sure what I can do to help her, Dad," Taylor said, starting to feel panicked. She felt like she'd just lost everything. "I really wish I could be there… I could come—"

"I don't think it'd be a good idea," her father said. "The doctors don't want to overwhelm her more."

Taylor's heart felt like it was being squeezed in a vise.

"I was sitting here with her," Taylor's dad said. "And I got this really bad feeling, like I wasn't really me. She just… I don't know. Maybe she's trying to figure out who I am."

Taylor's breath caught in her throat. She wanted to cry, but she couldn't. She wanted to scream. "Dad, I'm so sorry…"

"It's okay," he said, though he sounded like he was on the verge of tears. "It's not your fault. I know you're doing everything you can. I know you're doing everything you're allowed to do. I just… I just feel like we're losing her all over again, and I don't know how to fix it."

"I'm so sorry, Dad," Taylor said. "I wish I could help, but I don't know what else to do."

"I know," he said. "I'm sorry I called you about this. I know it's probably bad timing."

"It's not. I'll always have time for Angie. I'm working a hard case right now, but if she wakes up, and she asks for me… I'll be there. And Dad, I'm sorry you and Mom have to go through this again."

She just wanted to go back and fix everything, to rewrite time, to change everything so she never had to feel pain like this again.

"Taylor—" her dad said, and his voice broke. Taylor had never heard him sound so broken. "It's okay. I love you. I love you. I'll see you soon. I promise."

"Okay," Taylor said, her voice barely audible. "I love you too. I'll see you soon."

Taylor hung up, then stared into the black screen of her phone. Everything was falling apart. Finding Angie was supposed to be the solution to all the pain she and her parents had felt over the years…

But Taylor couldn't give up. Angie was still traumatized and recovering. She would get better. Taylor needed to see her in person. Maybe she could fix everything then. But if the doctor thought it was best for Angie to not be overwhelmed, then Taylor would keep her distance for now.

Taylor looked down the hallway to see Wesley running over to her, looking panicked.

"What's wrong?" she asked.

"Another murder," Wesley said, his face pale. "They found another body."

***

Taylor felt her heart race as they reached the scene. Another murder. It was all too familiar—the suburban street, the family homes… That was because this was the exact same street the previous victim, Isabel, had escaped the killer on.

Taylor could hardly believe what she was seeing as she and Wesley hurried up the sidewalk, toward the area where a house was barred off by caution tape. She was worried it was Isabel. That he'd come back to claim her. But it didn't make sense. They'd sent an officer to guard her. How could this happen?

As they drew closer, Taylor could see Detective Reynolds stationed at the corner of the house. He looked tired and stressed—likely because he was dealing with the press and investigating a murder on his watch.

Taylor's heart raced as she thought about Isabel. They'd said she was guarded… But now it seemed like that hadn't been enough. She had to find out what happened.

She motioned for Wesley to stop, then peered around the police tape to get a better view of the scene.

At the side of somebody's house, there was a body. Blood seeped into the earth and grass around it.

But it wasn't Isabel.

It was a man's body.

A young man, probably the same age as Isabel. He was dressed in black pants and a black sweater that was unbuttoned.

Taylor's heart skipped a beat.

"But… no," she said out loud. "This doesn't make sense."

The killer went after women. That had been the MO they'd been working with.

But now Taylor was supposed to believe he went after men too? And in broad daylight?

This changed everything—again. Taylor's head spun like she was on a carnival ride.

She was sick of pain. She was sick of death. She just wanted to get home to her family. She was trying to understand what she was seeing, to make sense of it, but it was all just blurs.

"Detective Reynolds!" Taylor called out, walking around the police line.

Wesley followed her, watching her with worried eyes.

The detective turned to her. "Special Agents Sage and Wesley," he said. "I'm glad you're here. You can tell me what you think once you've seen the scene, because I'm baffled."

He led them toward the body. Taylor couldn't take her eyes off it. This was worse than anything she could have imagined.

The man's throat had been slit, and there was blood all around him. It looked like he'd been killed just moments ago.

Taylor didn't want to believe this was happening again—but it was clear the killer had come back for another victim. But why return to the same street? Why did it have to be here—and why choose a new victim?

Taylor thought back to her earlier theory—that these were crimes of opportunity. The killer saw a house and a man. And he chose that setting to kill his next victim.

But this wasn't what she'd been thinking. She hadn't been thinking that the killer was just going to kill somebody else—she'd been thinking he would only kill a new victim in a new neighborhood.

This was bigger than that. This was a manhunt. The killer was still on the move.

"What do you make of it?" Taylor asked, turning to Reynolds.

"No idea," Reynolds said. "I was thinking he'd be some sick person harassing and killing women, but this… changes things."

Taylor looked at Wesley, who stared down at the scene with a grim look on his face. Their eyes locked for a moment, but they both turned away. Taylor wondered if Wesley was feeling the same way—that this was all their fault.

This young man had lost his life because they hadn't done their jobs right.

The pain was returning now, the way it always did when something bad happened. And Taylor knew this wasn't going to be the last time.

She needed a moment. She needed to collect herself. So she stormed away from the scene, and away from Wesley, to be alone.

CHAPTER TWENTY ONE

Taylor held her hand to her sweaty forehead beneath her bangs as she paced down the sidewalk. This was a disaster. Not only was another person dead, but the MO had completely shifted, and Taylor had no idea where to go from here.

She was supposed to be finding the killer, but she kept getting knocked down. She felt helpless. Was she supposed to just give in and let the killer win?

She thought about what Belasco had said when she'd visited her the other day. The Tower card…

"This represents a period of change, unexpected problems and unfortunate situations that may knock you down, but you need to get back up. Take this time to decide what you really want. The old way of doing things is no longer working for you. You're going to have to do something new."

Maybe this was relevant to the case, but Taylor couldn't think of the "new" thing Belasco was referring to. What could she do? She had no profile for the guy, no evidence at any of the scenes.

Up the street, the crime scene was still in full force: police everywhere, and forensics had just arrived in a van. Taylor saw Wesley step onto the sidewalk and look down the street to spot her, but she turned away. She needed a moment. Thankfully, Wesley stayed over there and continued talking to the officers.

In a moment like this, where everything was flipped upside down, Taylor would usually go to her father for help. But with everything going on with Angie, she knew she couldn't ask that of him now.

She needed to keep a positive attitude, even though she didn't feel it.

She thought back to Angie, recovering in the hospital. She thought of how Angie might see Taylor now that they were both adults. Taylor wanted to be someone Angie could be proud of. She didn't want to be an FBI agent who couldn't even save a life.

Taylor felt her phone vibrate in her pocket, and she pulled it out, hoping it was Angie or literally any good news—but it was from her ex-husband, Ben, of all people. His text read: *Taylor, I heard you found your sister alive... that's incredible. I'm so happy for you. Call me if you can, okay?*

Taylor felt sick just seeing Ben's name. He was the last person she wanted to hear from right now, even if his words were kind. They'd been married for years, but it went downhill fast, and now everything was too painful to think about.

But she needed to get her head on straight. Maybe what Belasco said could be significant—Taylor just didn't know how yet.

She began making her way back over to the crime scene. Wesley broke away from the officers he was talking to and met with Taylor on the sidewalk.

"Hey, you okay?" he asked.

"Yeah, I'm fine," Taylor said. "Just... needed to breathe."

"You sure?"

She nodded, but she was still feeling shaky. She didn't want to be this way around Wesley—it was bad enough that everyone else seemed to think she was a loose cannon, but Wesley was becoming her rock.

"I'm fine," she said again. "I know I want to be strong and calm here, but it's hard."

"You're going through some tough stuff," Wesley said. "What happened to Angie..."

"I don't want to talk about it right now," Taylor said. "But thanks."

He looked at her, his brow furrowed. "I know, Taylor... but we need to talk through this. We're going to solve this case. We'll find the killer."

"I know." Taylor sighed and looked away. "Any evidence?"

"I don't know," Wesley said. "I saw the same things you did at the scene, but I don't know what to make of it."

Taylor wanted to keep some distance, but she didn't want to be alone. She always felt better when she had Wesley around.

Taylor shrugged. "I need to talk to Reynolds," she said. "Wanna come with? You can help me out with the details."

Wesley nodded. "I'm good with that."

Taylor led him back to the police tape, which had been moved down to the sidewalk, and they stood there, watching the detectives and the crime scene team work.

Taylor saw Detective Reynolds meet with a group of officers and shake his head. He was standing in front of the house, and he pointed to the spot where the killer had cut the young man's throat.

Seeing Taylor, Reynolds nodded at her, his face serious. He came over to join her and Wesley on the lawn, off to the side of the crime scene.

"Any news?" Taylor asked again, her voice low.

Reynolds let out a sigh. "We've got a couple sets of prints," Reynolds said. "But they could be anyone's. This is someone's house, after all. And no prints were left at the other scenes, so… I'm not optimistic."

Taylor nodded, feeling defeated. She had this terrible feeling that the killer was just about to jump out at her.

"What do we know about the victim?" Taylor asked. "Is he a local?"

"Yes," Reynolds said. "Just out of college, and he had a bright future ahead of him."

Reynolds shook his head. "It's tragic, really… this could have been such a happy time for him. Seems like it was the wrong place at the wrong time."

Taylor nodded. This really was looking like a crime of opportunity.

But as she looked at the crime scene, another thought struck her.

The other women had been killed in alleyways, lured in. According to Isabel, with a voice and a creepy doll.

But apparently, the killer had lured this guy over to this house, in broad daylight. Did he use the same method?

Taylor stepped over the caution tape and approached the scene again, leaving Wesley to watch. The officers photographing the scene stepped aside to allow Taylor through.

She eyed up the grassy area, next to the pool of blood. It was hard to say if the police had disturbed the scene too much, but Taylor had a gut feeling she was looking for something significant. Something to do with that doll.

And that was when she saw it.

She knelt down in the grass.

Right near the wall, beside the fence that led into the backyard, there was a slight imprint in the grass. The blades were bent.

Maybe the doll was placed here.

Taylor stood up, squinting as she looked around, imagining the scene. Where did he hide when he lured the man out? How did he do it?

Taylor walked into the backyard to a nearby tree and stared up at the surprisingly tall beech, a few of its branches broken off. She imagined the killer's face, setting up the victim, the doll…

He might have crouched down here, right under this tree. Or maybe he hid behind the corner of the house and lured the victim with his voice that way.

The voice…

An idea struck her. Taylor thought about Belasco's words, about trying something "new." Maybe she'd been going about this the wrong way. She'd been looking into people who could alter their voices—but they had a live victim who had actually heard the voice in real life.

Maybe she'd even be able to identify it if she heard it.

CHAPTER TWENTY TWO

Taylor sat on the couch at Isabel's house with Wesley sitting beside her. Isabel was in a chair across the coffee table, her arms folded, while Taylor had her phone out.

"Okay, let's try this one," Taylor said. She turned the phone's speaker on and clicked to the recording of the voice.

"Hello," the voice said, in a smooth, high-pitched tone, very cartoonish. "My name is Barry. I'm here to help you."

It was an audition from a voice actor's profile online. Isabel shot Taylor a frown and shook her head.

"That's not the voice I heard."

"We'll try something else," Taylor said. "If we can't get a match, we'll have to start looking elsewhere, but…"

But Taylor had a strong feeling that this could lead them somewhere good. This could be the "new" thing Belasco was referencing in the reading. Taylor's anxiety rose as she found another local voice actor online and played his clip.

"Hi!" the voice droned, in a tone that couldn't have been more different from Barry's. "I'm Elliot, and I'm here to help!"

The new clip was thicker, more high-pitched, and sounded more like a guy in his forties, but definitely not Barry.

"This one doesn't sound like it either," Isabel said solemnly. "I'm so sorry, I wish I could be more helpful…"

Taylor shot Wesley a look, and he just nodded. He was being quiet; normally, he was a lot more vocal on cases, but Taylor had the feeling he was still distracted—maybe by the conversation they'd had earlier.

"Let's try another," Taylor said. She wasn't willing to give up so easily, even if they'd already tried twenty voice actors with no results.

"Of course, but…" Isabel bit her lip. "Is it okay if we maybe take a short break? I could whip up some lunch for you two."

"Oh, no, we couldn't accept that," Taylor said.

"Please," Isabel said. "I insist. Really. It'd be my pleasure."

Taylor glanced over at Wesley. He nodded. Taylor knew how his appetite could be, and they hadn't stopped for breakfast. He was probably starving, although Taylor was used to not eating—not because she didn't want to. She sometimes just got so wrapped up in her work that she forgot.

"That would be great, Isabel," Taylor said. "You're very kind. Thank you."

Isabel stood up and headed for the kitchen, muttering about how timing was everything and that she was happy to cook for two FBI agents.

Taylor and Wesley sat in silence for a few moments. They both had an appetite, but Taylor wasn't sure if she wanted anything. She felt like she was grasping at straws with this case, and there wasn't anything else they could do—not yet.

"Do you want something to drink?" Wesley asked eventually. "I can go get us some coffee."

"No, you should stay here. I'm sure Isabel has coffee."

"Yeah," Wesley muttered, wiping his hands on his pants. "She's a nice girl."

Taylor looked at him. Wesley definitely seemed different than usual. He'd been… distant. "Are you okay?" she asked him.

"Yeah," he said. "Just… want to get this wrapped up."

Taylor felt her nerves pinch. Suddenly she got the feeling that Wesley was uncomfortable with her. That maybe after this, he'd want to request a change in partners. Taylor would understand. If there was tension between them—romantic or sexual or otherwise—then that would be a distraction at best, and wildly unprofessional at worst. But…

Taylor didn't want to be apart from him. They worked well together. They had great chemistry and they always got the job done.

If they were having a problem, there were other ways they could deal with it. They didn't have to split apart. Right?

Taylor glanced into the kitchen, where the warm, inviting scent of food was cooking. Isabel was stirring a pot on the stove and the sound of sizzling meat and boiling water filled the air. The kitchen was small, but it had all the necessary appliances: a refrigerator, a stove, a sink, and cupboards. There was a window, but it was covered in a heavy curtain. Taylor could see the sun shining through the gaps.

She turned to Wesley. She didn't want to keep this sudden anxiety in.

"Wes," she started, and his gray eyes locked on hers. "What are you thinking about for after the case?"

“What do you mean?” Again, he wiped his palms on his pants. It was not like Wesley to be so nervous. He’d always been headstrong and brash.

“I mean, with us,” Taylor said. “Do you want to keep being partners?”

He blinked and looked away, pretending to look at the file on the coffee table.

“Wes, I don’t want to be apart from you. I don’t want you to leave either, but I don’t want to feel like there’s tension between us. We’ve always worked well together.”

“Of course,” he said. “Always. You’re a great partner, Taylor. I’m always happy to work with you.”

“If it was up to me,” Taylor said, “I’d want us to stay together.”

“I don’t want to split up either,” he said. “I think we should be partners. Not just partners, really. Friends too.”

Taylor’s heart warmed. So everything was okay. “You still seem distant though, and like your head isn’t really in the work,” Taylor commented.

“Yeah. It’s just these… feelings. They sort of came out of nowhere. Guess I wasn’t prepared.” He glanced in the kitchen. Isabel was still working away. Wesley’s eyes met Taylor’s again, and she couldn’t help but feel a fire in her chest. “Look, Taylor, it’s about more than just that we’re partners. We’re technically allowed to date whoever we want, no law or rules against it. But… you’re still going through a divorce, and I can’t put that pressure on you.”

Taylor looked away. Right—the divorce. It wasn’t like she even had feelings for Ben anymore. Seeing him on her phone earlier had just pissed her off, if anything.

But she understood where Wesley was coming from. Taylor was going through a lot. And this was as unexpected for her as it was him.

“I know,” Taylor agreed. “I don’t know if this is a good idea. I’m not sure I want to go back to dating anyone.” She sighed.

Wesley reached for her hand and squeezed it, a gentle reassuring squeeze that made Taylor’s throat close up.

“I don’t want to date anyone either. I want to keep working with you.”

Taylor wanted to say she wanted the same thing. She wanted to say that she wanted to keep working with him. She wanted to say that even if she never wanted to date again, she wanted to work with him. She pressed her lips together.

"It's okay, Taylor," Wesley said. "I've been on the job a long time, and I can tell when things aren't okay. It's okay."

Taylor looked up, and with a sigh, she put her face in his hands. "You're right. We'll figure it out. I'm sorry. I'm really sorry," she told him.

"Don't be sorry. I'm sorry. I can be a real ass sometimes. I shouldn't have hugged you like that, I just… wanted to protect you."

Taylor laughed, but there was a kind of sadness to it. She'd felt so safe with him in that moment. She didn't regret anything. "You know, I've never really dated any of the partners I've worked with in the past," she said. "It's always been important for me to keep that part of my personal life separate from my professional life. Plus, I was married for so long. Is it that way for you?"

Wesley didn't say anything. Taylor wasn't sure what to make of that. Had he fallen for another partner before? For some reason, the thought made Taylor's stomach sink.

"All done!" Isabel exclaimed, coming into the room with bowls of soup and sandwiches on a tray.

"Here you go." She put the two bowls down with the sandwiches, sliding Taylor and Wesley each a plate.

"Thank you, Isabel," Taylor said. "We appreciate you cooking for us. You really did not have to."

"Are you kidding? I insisted," Isabel said. "You two are helping me out. Plus, cooking helps me keep my mind off what happened."

Taylor nodded. She understood that. Although it felt strange to accept food from a witness.

But then she looked at the steaming mounds of food that Isabel had brought, and she knew Isabel was telling the truth. She was polite and helping them out. That was all.

Taylor sat down and started eating, her appetite coming back with a vengeance. She knew it was just a matter of time before her mind returned to the case. She would get back to it. She just needed to take a break. She needed to stop thinking and just allow herself to feel for a moment. Taylor knew her biggest flaw was that she thought too much about everything.

The food was delicious. The soup was rich and the bread tasted like home. Wesley was finished within moments, while Taylor ate slower. Isabel smiled at them as she cleared the table.

"I can't thank you enough for everything you're doing," Taylor said. "It really wasn't necessary."

Isabel stopped what she was doing. She looked over at them, her blue eyes full of gratitude. "It's not necessary to thank me. I have to do what I can do to help. I don't want what happened to me and that poor man, plus those other girls, to happen to anyone else."

Taylor nodded. "I'm glad you made it out okay. This was nice, but we really do need to focus back on the case."

"You're right, I'm sorry," Isabel said. "I just needed a little mental health break. Let's keep going."

Isabel cleared away the dishes and came back in, sitting back in the chair, and Taylor refocused on her phone. She went to the next voice actor—a man named Leonard Phelps, who did cartoon voice acting for children's shows remotely. Taylor played a clip, and Leonard's voice filled the room. It was a soundbite of a role he'd played in a recent kids' show.

"Hi, everyone, I'm Binky!"

Taylor expected Isabel not to react, considering they'd played two dozen of these so far and nothing had come up.

But a strange, haunted look came over her face.

"Isabel?" Taylor asked.

"It's close," Isabelle said. She became eerily pale. "No—that is the voice. It has to be."

"Are you sure?" Taylor's heart raced as she leaned forward.

Isabel nodded. She looked like she'd seen a ghost, just hearing that voice again. Taylor's heart went out to her—and what she'd been through.

Taylor went onto her phone and searched Leonard Phelps further. And what came up made her blood run cold. There was an article titled:

BELOVED CHILD ACTOR CHARGED WITH DOMESTIC VIOLENCE, FIRED BY AGENT.

It was a tabloid article from a few years ago—about his first wife. Taylor stared at the image.

The woman looked a lot like Isabel. The two were almost identical. The woman had a similar build, though with a bit of a figure, and she had long, curly, light brown hair. She looked to be in her late twenties or early thirties.

It couldn't be. But she had to be. Taylor's heart pounded in her chest. She looked at Isabel again. The resemblance really was uncanny.

But it still didn't add up. If Leonard was their guy, and he was obsessed with a woman who looked like Isabel… why did he kill the random man? And what about the other two women? Then again, if

Isabel identified him as the voice, then that was huge. It could unravel everything.

Taylor didn't have the answers, not yet. But this Leonard Phelps guy was worth paying a visit.

CHAPTER TWENTY THREE

Wesley needed to get his head together.

As he and Taylor crept up to Leonard Phelps's house, he reminded himself not to get caught up in his feelings. He couldn't get involved with a partner romantically…

Not again.

He stared at Taylor's back as she walked ahead of him, and he shook the thoughts away. They were at a damn suspect's house. Now was not the time to think about how close he'd felt to Taylor Sage earlier. How much he'd wanted to take her pain away. *Focus, Wesley. You're a better agent than this.*

He had to prove that to himself. It was getting later in the day now, and the afternoon sky was cloudy. Leaves were slowly dying on the trees around them, bringing the feel of Halloween. Wesley's daughter loved Halloween more than any holiday of the year.

Wesley's eyes swept over the small, shabby house as they walked up the driveway. It was a rickety, weather-beaten structure with peeling paint and faded curtains. The windows were covered in dust and cobwebs, and the door was ajar. But there was a car in the driveway and beer bottles littering the front porch, so someone must have been home.

Taylor and Wesley looked at each other as they approached the house. This was it—the guy who had killed three women. They could feel their adrenaline pumping through their veins, and Taylor's hands started to tremble slightly.

They took a deep breath and stepped forward. Leonard Phelps was standing in the doorway, swaying unsteadily. He looked drunk and angry, and it took him a few moments to notice them walking up to him.

"Who are you?" he slurred, his voice thick with alcohol. "Answer me or I'll call the police!"

Taylor took a step forward, holding out her badge. "I'm with the FBI," she said firmly. "We're here to talk to you."

Leonard Phelps's face went pale, and he stumbled backwards into the house. "What about?" he cried, clinging to the doorframe for support. "I'm a little busy right now!"

"We just need to ask a few questions. It won't take long," Taylor said, trying to keep her voice even.

"All right, all right, pull my leg why don't ya…"

Leonard swayed slightly, but Taylor and Wesley followed him in anyway. They found themselves in a dark room, lit only by the light through a few windows that were boarded up. The furniture was stacked helter-skelter, and clothes littered the floor. The room smelled musty and dirty, and it made Wesley's stomach churn.

Wesley looked around, his eyes sweeping the room. A movie was playing in the background on an old TV. It was an old, grainy flick of "Binky" in an old kids' show. Wesley felt his whole body tense.

"Are you Leonard Phelps?" Wesley asked.

"Aren't you supposed to be the FBI agent?" Phelps said, taking a swig of his beer. He chuckled. "Yeah, that's me. What do you want?"

Wesley exchanged an uneasy look with Taylor. Something told him this could go south fast. This guy was clearly wasted. Maybe to celebrate his earlier kill?

"We just have a few questions to ask," Wesley said, keeping his voice smooth.

Leonard took another swig of beer, then held his hand out to them. His breath smelled like alcohol and cigarettes. He looked at them expectantly. "Well, go on then."

"Where were you two nights ago?" Taylor asked.

"I was here, at home," Leonard said, his voice slurring slightly. He took another swig of his beer, then held the bottle out to them. "Want one?"

Wesley shook his head, but Taylor took the bottle and pretended to take a drink before handing it back to him.

"You were home?" she asked, trying to sound casual. "What were you doing?"

"Watching TV, like I am now," he said. He gestured to the old TV in the corner. "What does it look like I was doing?"

"And you didn't leave the house at all? Not even to go outside for a smoke?" Wesley asked. He was watching Leonard closely, trying to gauge his reaction.

Leonard's eyes narrowed and he glared at Wesley. "I told you, I was here at home," he said angrily. "Now why don't you just leave me alone?"

Phelps's eyes narrowed and he took a step closer to Wesley, his hand tightening around the beer bottle. "I was right here," he snarled, his voice filled with anger. "And I'm not going to tell you where I was or what I was doing. Now get the hell out of my house!"

He raised his arm and threw the beer bottle at Wesley, who ducked just in time. It shattered against the wall, sending shards of glass flying everywhere.

Wesley's blood instantly burned. He went to go subdue Leonard's drunk ass—but Leonard lunged forward, swinging his arm wildly. Wesley stepped back, trying to avoid a hit from the guy.

"Hey!" Taylor cried, moving forward to restrain Leonard. "Calm down, we're just trying to ask you a few questions!"

"I don't have to answer to you!" Leonard shouted, struggling against Taylor's grip. "Get out of my house!"

With one final, powerful shove, Leonard managed to break free from Taylor's grasp and send her sprawling backwards. He staggered toward Wesley, grabbing another beer bottle off the coffee table and brandishing it like a weapon.

And that was more than enough for Wesley.

He pulled out his gun and pointed it straight at Leonard. "Leonard Phelps, drop the weapon. Now."

A moment of clarity seemed to pass over Leonard as he processed what was happening. He dropped the bottle and put his hands up.

"All right, all right," he said, his voice shaking. "I'm sorry. I didn't mean to."

"Turn around and put your hands on the wall," Wesley ordered.

Leonard complied, and Wesley quickly patted him down, searching for any other weapons. When he was satisfied that Leonard was no longer a threat, he turned him around and read him his Miranda rights.

"You have the right to remain silent," Wesley began. "Anything you say can and will be used against you in a court of law. You have the right to an attorney. If you cannot afford one, one will be provided for you. Do you understand these rights as they have been read to you?"

"Yes," Leonard muttered.

"Good," Wesley said. He turned to Taylor, who looked frazzled and exhausted. "Let's go."

***

Wesley didn't want to waste any more time. Leonard was taken to the local precinct for interrogation, where he was placed in a small, cramped room with a table and two chairs. Wesley and Taylor sat across from him, both of them looking stern and serious.

"Now, Mr. Phelps," Wesley began. "I'm going to ask you again. Where were you two nights ago?"

"I told you, I was at home," Leonard said, his voice slightly slurring. He looked down at the table, avoiding eye contact. "I didn't do nothing—I don't know what this is even about. I need another drink…"

"I'm sorry, Mr. Phelps, but you're going to have to sober up before we can continue this conversation," Wesley said. He sighed and shook his head. "Two nights ago, a woman was brutally murdered in an alleyway downtown. We have reason to believe that you may have been involved."

"What the hell are you talking about?" Leonard slurred. His eyes were rolling in his head. This guy was still so drunk. And not helpful at all.

They were getting nowhere.

"Get me another drink," Leonard muttered. He put his head down flat on the table.

"I think we're done here," Wesley said, standing up.

He turned to leave the room, but not before giving Leonard one last, long look. He looked like a man who was lost—a man who had given up on life. There was something about him that made Wesley feel pity, despite everything.

Wesley left the room and Taylor followed close behind him. They both sighed in relief, glad to be out of there.

"That was a bust," Wesley said, running a hand through his hair. "He's still too drunk to be of any use to us."

"What do you think?" Taylor asked. "He's our guy?"

"I don't know," Wesley said. "It seems plausible. He clearly doesn't have an alibi, and his voice matched the one Isabel heard."

Wesley crossed his arms. The more he thought of it, the more sure he was. Leonard was a pathetic, drunk, bitter man. It wouldn't be a stretch at all for him to start killing people as some sort of revenge, or even just to lash out at the world.

"It's gotta be him," Wesley said.

"But what do we have to go on?" Taylor asked. "We don't have any concrete evidence linking him to the murder."

"I know," Wesley said. "But he's all we've got right now. We need to watch him closely. Hopefully, he'll slip up and give us something."

Taylor looked down, brows pinched. Wesley knew that look. Despite everything pointing at Leonard, it seemed like Taylor didn't buy it. From what he'd seen so far, Taylor's gut instincts were almost always right.

Hell, apparently she'd solved a two-decade-old missing persons case on a "hunch," although he knew it was way more than that.

"What are you thinking, Sage?" Wesley asked.

"It's just…" She trailed off. "Something doesn't feel right."

"Okay, what is it?"

"I don't know. I know Isabel identified the voice. But she also said it was close, not necessarily the exact same. And something about her testimony is standing out to me."

"And what's that?" Wesley asked. He wasn't totally following. This still seemed like a fairly done deal to him.

"She said the killer yelled at her to stop," Taylor said. "After he'd already been caught, he was still using the voice. Why would he keep using it if he'd already been found out? He already lured her in with the child's voice, so what I don't get is why he'd continue to use it."

Wesley nodded. He'd never thought about that. "Well, he could just be a sicko," Wesley said. "He could have wanted to continue using the voice even if he was caught. And under the circumstances, it seems like he'd want to finish her off with the same voice. Maybe he was just in a rush to finish and get out of there."

"Maybe," Taylor said. "It's just…I don't want to jump to any conclusions. We've pinned all our hopes on Leonard, and if we're wrong, we could be risking letting the real killer go. I want to be certain before we jump to any conclusions."

Wesley nodded, processing what Taylor was telling him. It made sense, in a way. They couldn't afford to make a mistake.

"You're right, Taylor," he said. "We have to be sure. So what are you thinking?"

"We'll keep Leonard here," Taylor said. "But we'll keep looking." She paused. Wesley listened intently, eager to hear her thoughts. "Maybe we've been going about this wrong," Taylor said. "Maybe we're not looking for a voice actor. Maybe we're looking for somebody whose voice is just always like that."

"You mean somebody with a messed up voice?" Wesley asked.

Taylor nodded. "Exactly. And I think I have an idea of where to start looking."

CHAPTER TWENTY FOUR

Taylor clacked her fingers across the keyboard of her laptop, back at the hotel room. She was at the edge of solving this case—she could feel it in her bones. She just needed to get there. She was online, looking for any information about any children—or adults—with unique or different voices published online. Nothing concrete had come up yet, but Taylor had a strong feeling she'd get somewhere soon.

Through the window of the hotel, the sun was beginning to set, a deep orange, like a molten lava, slowing dropping behind the buildings and trees. The sky was a deep blue, like a sapphire, and the stars were beginning to come out. The hotel was in the middle of the city, and the noise of the traffic was beginning to die down. The lights were coming on in the buildings and the streets, and the people were starting to come out.

Wesley wasn't back yet—he'd gone out to grab them some dinner. Now alone, Taylor glanced at the bed they'd slept in last night—the bed he'd held her in. Her throat tightened as she thought about what might happen if they had to spend another night here. Taylor hoped that wouldn't be the case—she wanted to solve this case and get home to Angie. She felt better about where she and Wesley were at in their partnership after the conversation they'd had. But still, Taylor couldn't help but feel anxious at the thought of what was to come.

Her eyes went back to her screen—there was a hit.

Taylor clicked on the link, and the article popped up. It was about a strange anomaly in a girl's voice a couple years ago, in a small town near Flyway City. But Taylor was looking for a male—Isabel had clearly identified the killer as a man. So this was a no-go.

There had to be something else…

Suddenly, Taylor's phone rang, and she whipped it out.

It was her mom.

"Mom?" Taylor answered.

"Hi, sweetie."

It was good to hear her voice.

"How's Angie?"

"Still sedated and sleeping, unfortunately," her mom said. "But I wanted to see how you're doing."

"I'm fine," Taylor said. "Just working on the case."

"Have you made any progress?" her mom asked.

"I think so. I think I'm close."

"That's so exciting," her mom said. "I know how you hate not being able to solve one of these cases."

"You know me too well." Taylor laughed. "But I'm getting close, I just know it. And my partner… he has my back."

Taylor's face warmed. She'd appreciated how Wesley was willing to listen to her earlier when she pitched the idea that Leonard wasn't their guy. Right now, Leonard was still in the drunk tank. Maybe he was their killer—but Taylor had to chase down this new lead.

"Your partner?" her mom asked. "You haven't told us about him."

"Oh, he's just Wesley," Taylor said. "He's a good guy."

"Ah." Taylor could practically hear her mom's smile on the other end of the phone.

"Is he cute?"

"Mom," Taylor said, flustered. "Is now really the time for that?" Her face was on fire. But her mom had always been overly interested in Taylor's love life. It was meant to be supportive, of course.

"I'm sorry," her mom said. "I just… needed a distraction as I've been waiting for Angie to wake up. I needed to have a normal conversation with my girl."

Taylor sighed. She couldn't fault her mom for that. "Yes, Mom. He's cute."

"Oh, that's nice," her mom said. "Do you have a lot of cases that you work together?"

"It's kind of a work-in-progress," Taylor said. "It's only our third case together. But we have a lot of faith in each other, and we work well together."

"That's nice," her mom said. "I'm glad you have someone."

"Well, he has me, too."

"Of course," her mom said with a laugh. "I want to make sure you know you have me as well."

"You're my best friend, Mom," Taylor said, smiling. She meant that. She'd never had much room in her life for actual friendships, but her mom had always been there. Same with her dad.

"How's Dad holding up?" Taylor asked.

"He's seen better days, of course," her mom said. "But he's hanging on. He's here almost all the time."

"I'm sure Angie would be happy to know he's there," Taylor said. She'd love to see her dad again. He was always so calm, no matter what was going on.

"Are you coming back soon?" her mom asked.

"I hope so," Taylor said. "I'm doing everything in my power to get back to Angie as soon as possible. But the doctor said I should keep some distance for a bit too."

"I know you want to be there for her when she wakes up," her mom said. "And we want you to be there for her, too. We love you, honey. We'll sort everything out."

"I love you, too."

"I'll let you get back to work now," her mom said. "I'll call you if anything comes up."

"Thanks, Mom."

Taylor ended the call just as Wesley came back into the room with fast food in hand. The smell of grease and onions filled the air, and she could see the steam rising from the paper-wrapped burgers. Her stomach growled, and she realized she was starving.

"How are you holding up?" Wesley asked.

"Good. Thanks for doing this," Taylor said.

Wesley set the food down on the table and sat down next to her, handing her a burger and fries. She took a bite, and the flavors exploded in her mouth. Grease, onions, ketchup, mustard, pickles, and beef all mingled together in a delicious dance.

It was silence between them as they ate, but it was a comfortable silence. They were both lost in their own thoughts, thinking about the case. The silence was broken only by the sound of their food wrappers crinkling and the occasional creak of the chair as one of them shifted. The air in the room was thick with tension and anticipation. They both knew that they were close to solving the case, but they weren't quite sure how to put all of the pieces together. They would have to go over everything again, from the beginning. But for now, they just sat in silence and ate their dinner.

After they finished eating, Wesley leaned back in his chair and let out a long sigh. "This is one hell of a mess," he said.

Taylor nodded, her mind still racing. "I know," she said. "But I think I'm getting close."

"What do you mean?" Wesley asked, leaning forward slightly.

“I’ve been looking for anything online about people with unique or different voices,” Taylor explained. She went back onto her laptop and moved down to the next search result.

There was a study published by a psychiatrist in Flyway about a teenage boy who refused to speak in school, set about ten years ago. Maybe that wasn’t quite what Taylor was looking for; she wanted someone with a strange voice, not a mute. But something in the article caught her eye.

“The boy could speak, but he chose not to,” it read. “His voice was rather high-pitched, and it seemed he was ashamed to let others hear it.”

Interesting, Taylor thought.

“Wesley, check this out.” She turned the screen to him. Wesley leaned over to read the highlighted passage.

“Hmm,” he said. “It could mean something. It did happen here in Flyway.”

She kept reading the article, and it mentioned another thing that stood out to her:

“The boy’s mother worked at a toy shop, and it seemed like he’d always been attached to toys—particularly humanoid dolls.”

Taylor’s mind raced as she read the highlighted passage over and over again. She looked at Wesley, reading his expression. He nodded.

If this was true, it could be huge.

Taylor looked back at the screen. The study was published by one Dr. Frank Rubato. Taylor searched Frank online and found out that he had a practice that was still open here in town. It closed at six p.m.

If they hurried, they could still make it there.

“We should go talk to him,” Taylor said, grabbing her jacket and her keys. She had to check this out.

“It’s almost six now,” Wesley said. “But if he’s the one, we need to take this chance. He might be the key to this whole case.”

“Let’s go, then,” Taylor said. He got up and followed her out.

***

It was a short drive to Dr. Rubato’s office. It was downtown, close to the main street. They parked in front of the old brick building and walked inside. The building smelled like a hospital, and Taylor closed her eyes as she took a deep breath, in an attempt to stave off the anxiety that she knew would come in waves.

The office was a bit less clinical than she had expected. There were framed prints of sunflowers on the walls, and on the counter, a basket of plastic toys and coloring books were scattered about. The toys were meant for children, but Taylor knew that some adults needed to be entertained, too.

The receptionist was a pretty young woman with long brown hair. She was wearing a short, stylish dress with flirty platform sandals.

"Can I help you?" she asked.

"Is Dr. Rubato in?" Taylor asked, not revealing that they had some business with him.

"He's just finishing up with a patient," the receptionist said. "Should be just a few minutes."

"Great," Wesley said. "We'll wait."

The receptionist nodded and sat back in her chair.

Taylor and Wesley took seats in the small waiting room. It was almost empty. The door opened, and a woman in a black dress walked out of the office, clutching a folder in her hand.

"Thank you so much, Dr. Rubato," she said. "You've been such a help to my son."

"Of course, ma'am," Dr. Rubato said. "Jim is a really bright kid. If we can get over this hump, I know he'll have a bright future."

As the woman left, Taylor and Wesley stood up. Taylor walked over to Dr. Rubato as he was about to go into his office and took out her badge.

"Dr. Rubato?"

He turned to them and frowned, then saw the badge.

"We're with the FBI," Taylor said. "Do you mind if we chat for a minute?"

Dr. Rubato was a handsome man, with olive skin and deep brown eyes. In his early fifties, he was balding, but his face still looked young.

"FBI?" he asked. "Why are you here?"

"We're investigating a murder," Wesley said. "You might be able to help us."

"What do you need?" Dr. Rubato asked. "If I can help, of course I'm willing. Why don't you two come into my office?"

Wesley and Taylor followed him into the office. It was small and cluttered. Two desks were pushed up against the wall, and on them were stacks of papers, comic books, and classic books. *The Great Gatsby*, *The Catcher in the Rye*. Dr. Rubato sat behind his desk while Taylor and Wesley took the two chairs in front.

"So," Dr. Rubato said, "how can I help?"

"You published a study online about ten years ago about a boy who refused to speak," Taylor said. "Do you recall?"

Dr. Rubato nodded slowly. "Oh, yes… I remember well."

"You mentioned the boy could speak, but he refused to because his voice sounded so high."

"That's right," Dr. Rubato said. "He was a troubled young man. I was assigned to work with him via his high school guidance counselor."

Taylor looked at Wesley. He nodded at her, probably thinking the same thing.

"Can you tell us more about this boy?" Taylor asked. "Who he was, his home life, if he was ever… violent."

Dr. Rubato leaned back in his chair, a look of concern on his face. "I am not supposed to give out this kind of information. You know this."

"It's a lot to ask," Taylor said. "But this is an FBI investigation, and we have reason to believe this young man could be a person of interest."

"But there's no way he could have anything to do with a murder," Dr. Rubato said. "Right?"

"We're not saying he does," Taylor said. "We're just following up on every lead."

"I understand that," Dr. Rubato said. "Let me just pull up his file."

Dr. Rubato moved over to his desk and opened up his computer. He typed some keys, and a file came up on the screen. "Here he is," he said. "Cole Phearson. I worked with him for about a year, and we made a lot of progress."

"Did you go to his home?" Taylor asked.

"Yes, I did," Dr. Rubato said. "He was a smart kid on paper, but he didn't talk at all at school. I first heard his voice by accident when I was visiting his home. He was a troubled young man. His parents weren't well off, and they were fighting a lot. He was beaten. His mother was a drug addict, and he was raised in a very abusive household."

"But he was still in high school," Taylor said. "Why wasn't he living with someone more suitable? Someone who could be a better parent?"

"His father was… very controlling," Dr. Rubato said. "I remember that much."

"And his mother?" Taylor asked.

"I don't know too much about her," Dr. Rubato said. "I wasn't around her enough. I get the sense that she just gave up after a while."

"Do you know if Cole ever talked to his father about the abuse?" Taylor asked. "Did he ever talk to either of his parents about anything?"

"He didn't speak to anyone at school," Dr. Rubato said. "He was a very introverted young man. And as far as I know, he didn't speak to his parents much, either."

"Did you have any other interactions with him after your sessions?" Taylor asked.

"No," Dr. Rubato said. "He was going to come to my office a few times, but he never showed up."

"Did he give you a reason?"

"He told his guidance counselor that he was having some trouble at school and didn't have time. And by told, I mean he wrote it down on paper. That was how he communicated. He did not know sign language, which was odd for somebody with mutism. That was the first flag to me that the boy really could speak, but just chose not to."

"Did you recommend that Cole be placed in foster care?" Taylor asked.

Dr. Rubato shook his head. "I couldn't. Cole's mother wanted him back, and she wanted him to live with his father. That was the only way he could stay home. I recommended that they do marriage counseling, but they didn't follow through. It was a very sad situation. I do think that Cole had some serious mental illnesses he was dealing with."

Taylor nodded, thinking on this. She'd seen these situations too many times. Not the mutism—that was new. But the fact that there was a child raised in an unstable environment. Oftentimes, this could lead to a very troubled adult.

Sometimes even a serial killer.

"And you never suspected Cole of anything violent?" Taylor asked.

Dr. Rubato hesitated.

"I don't want to say anything against the young man," Dr. Rubato said. "But I just had a feeling that… Cole was not quite right."

"And that was the last time you saw Cole?" Taylor asked.

Dr. Rubato nodded. "I have not known what happened to him since then."

"And I read in your article that his mother worked at a toy store," Taylor said. "You mentioned that he would be attached to dolls."

"That's right," Dr. Rubato said. "Cole had a tendency to… latch onto inanimate objects in general. I remember he had a cup he was very fond of, and one time he dropped and broke it, and he cried about it. But dolls, especially, he seemed to really adore. He would not bring them to school or anything, likely in fear of bullying, but on house visits I would see him carrying around a doll. Usually a female."

Taylor thought of Isabel's description of the doll. It was a match.

"It was odd, though," Rubato continued. "For such an abusive household, they lived in a nice family neighborhood. Not to say well-off parents can't abuse their children—they can, and it happens more often than one might think, but the situation always felt off."

"Do you remember what neighborhood it was?"

"I think it was Meadowdale," he said.

Taylor's heart stalled.

She looked over at Wesley.

He had the same realization on his face.

Meadowdale was the same street Isabel lived on—the same street that man had been killed on earlier.

***

Taylor and Wesley hurried back to the hotel room. As soon as they were back inside, Taylor dove for the laptop; she'd left it here when they went to Dr. Rubato's. But now, she needed to know everything she could about Cole Phearson—she needed everything the FBI had on him in their database.

Maybe they had some files that the public didn't have access to, like his school records. Maybe he had a criminal record. All the possibilities swam through Taylor's mind. This kid was their guy. She was sure of it.

She searched around for a bit, but there wasn't much. She ended up finding a picture of Cole. His brown hair was long, but he was clean-cut, and he looked like your average high school kid. But something in his eyes was… soulless.

She clicked on the history icon and searched around the internet. But there was nothing. Not even any social media accounts. Cole Phearson had ceased to exist after Dr. Rubato's study. He left high school and never worked a day in his life. He collected disability payments, but stayed off the grid.

It was too much of a coincidence. Cole once lived on the same street the victim earlier was killed on. But he didn't live there anymore. According to the database, his last known address was an apartment downtown. Taylor wrote it down; she was going to head there.

But first—she wanted to know more not only about Cole, but also his parents.

His mother was Linda Phearson. According to the database, she'd worked at a toy store.

The same toy store Mary Gibbons was killed beside.

His father was Gary Phearson. He was a janitor at an apartment building complex.

The same complex Emily Johnson had died beside.

Then, of course, the third victim had died on the same street Cole grew up on.

All at once, everything made sense. The location of each kill was personal to Cole. He had a connection to every single one.

The question now was: where would he go next?

CHAPTER TWENTY FIVE

Cole's shoes pounded the pavement as he moved quickly toward the hospital grounds, Betty tucked in the bag beside him. It was dark now, and the stars were out above. He knew it was a public place, but he'd gotten away with it on the street earlier—who could stop him now? No, he was sure he could get away with it. He would find someone for Betty here.

In the place where his father died.

Cole navigated the outside of the hospital grounds, his heart pounding in his chest. He passed by the west wing, where his father had taken his last breath. He could still see the ghost of his father in the chair, his skin pale and his eyes closed. He could still see the way his mother had collapsed when the doctor told them there was nothing more they could do. He could still hear the sound of her sobs echoing in the sterile hallways.

He shook his head to clear the memories and focused on the task at hand. He would find someone for Betty. He would not let her down.

He moved past a garden, to a more quiet, private part of the hospital, where visitors sometimes came out to smoke or get some fresh air. This was the place.

He remembered, a week before his father died, Cole had taken him out to this garden. The sun had been high in the sky, casting a warm glow on everything it touched. The flowers had been in full bloom, their petals reaching out to the sun. His father had told him, one last time, how worthless he was. The words had been like a knife, piercing his heart. He had wanted to scream, to tell his father that he was wrong, but the words had been stuck in his throat. He had just stood there, like a fool, while his father slumped in his wheelchair.

Cole had always dreamed of getting revenge.

His father had made fun of him his whole life for the way his voice sounded. Drunk, he would torture him verbally if he ever dared to speak.

When Cole was a small boy, he had thought that it was because his father was mocking him for being a sissy, for being a girl. The words had hurt, but they hadn't been the worst part. The worst part was the way his father had looked at him. He would stare at him with a twisted, sick smile on his face, like he was looking at something he'd rather see dead.

Cole had done his best to pretend that his father's words didn't bother him. He had tried to push them out of his head and live his life. But they had hurt, and they had brought him down, and they had continued to haunt him until the day he died. That was only two weeks ago, and the wounds were still so fresh.

He pulled the hood of his sweatshirt over his head so he couldn't be recognized. He passed by the benches and the trees, hiding from view. He pulled the bag out from under his sweatshirt and opened it. Betty was still there.

The night was calm and peaceful, with hardly a sound except for the occasional car rolling by on the street.

And the sound of Cole's breath as he shakily approached a bench. He put his hands on the bench, trying to steady himself as he sat down. He took out the vinyl gloves and put them on. He then took Betty out.

"Betty," he whispered to her. "Betty, I have something for you. I'm sure you'll like it."

He reached over to untie the blindfold he'd put on her, but she pushed his hand away with her cold little fingers. Her eyes opened and she looked at him coldly. But Cole couldn't help but smile. Betty was coming alive for him. She really did love him.

"Cole, you sound so lovely tonight," she said.

Cole licked his lips and smiled. "I could be useful," he said. "I could make you happy, Betty."

"Yes, you could," she agreed. "You could do a lot more than you think."

He was so happy. He hugged her tight. Betty, his beloved doll, had come to life.

"I wish I could have killed Father," he said to her, holding her, a tear in his eye. "I'm sorry I was too late. The heart failure took him fist. But I can make it right, Betty. I'll take someone else for you."

"Yes, you can," Betty said. "You will."

"I don't know who to take," Cole said. "I've been thinking about it all night in bed, and I don't know who to take. I need to find someone who is as evil as my father. Someone who deserves to die."

"No," Betty said. "You need to find someone who deserves to live."

Cole pulled her away and looked at her. "Someone who deserves to live?" he repeated, then he smiled. "Yes, of course. We'll save someone who is worth living. Whoever you want, Betty. I'll make you smile. I'll make you happy, just like you make me happy."

"I love you, Cole," she said.

"I love you too."

He kissed the top of her head before he put her down on the bench.

Then he disappeared into the bushes to watch, and wait, for his next victim to come.

CHAPTER TWENTY SIX

Taylor burst into Cole Phearson's apartment with her gun out, Wesley behind her.

It was a bachelor apartment, the windows covered by dark curtains. The living room was small and cramped, with a couch that had seen better days and a coffee table that was littered with take-out menus and empty beer bottles. The kitchen was even smaller, and the bed was just a mattress on the floor with a single pillow and a blanket. There was no art on the walls, no photos, no evidence that anyone lived there at all. It was a place to crash, nothing more.

But there was a smell that lingered in the air, making Taylor sick. The apartment was filled with the dusty, sour smell of old beer and a mix of body odor and sweat.

It was so small that Cole Phearson would have nowhere to hide. With her gun out, Taylor quickly surveyed the bathroom. It was just as empty as the living area, and there was no evidence that anyone had been in here. She went back over to Wesley, who was in the main area, looking around.

"He's not here," Taylor said.

Wesley walked over to the bed, stepped over a pile of clothes, and opened up the closet door. "It's clear in here," he said. He pointed to the window in the kitchen, which was cracked open.

They walked over to it and looked out. There was a fire escape right outside, and a view of the street.

"I doubt he saw us coming," Taylor said. "Maybe he's already looking for his next victim."

"Shit," Wesley said.

Taylor crossed her arms, thinking. Every location of a kill so far had been personal to Cole. If they could figure out where another "personal" spot was, maybe they could find out where he went.

And they were in his apartment. There had to be a clue somewhere.

Taylor began to search the apartment more carefully, looking for anything that could give her a clue about where Cole might have gone. She went through the drawers in the kitchen, sorted through the take-out menus and beer bottles on the coffee table, and even looked under the mattress. But she didn't find anything helpful.

She was about to give up when she noticed a notebook sticking out from under the pillow on the bed. It was well-worn, with pages that were dog-eared and covered in scribbles. Taylor flipped through it quickly, trying to make sense of the scrawl.

And then she saw it. A page with just a few words written in all capital letters: DAD FINALLY DIED… I'M SAD I COULDN'T DO IT MYSELF. BETTY IS MAD AT ME TOO. BUT… IT WAS HEART FAILURE. FINALLY. THEY TRIED TO SAVE HIM BUT THEY COULDN'T. GOOD RIDDANCE.

It was dated two weeks ago.

Cole's dad had recently died. That must have been why he was so angry, why he was lashing out. Taylor put the notebook down and sat on the bed, thinking.

If the dad died of heart failure, and "they" tried to save him, then he must have meant the hospital.

Taylor looked at Wesley, panic-stricken. "I think I know where he went."

***

Taylor's heart pounded the walls of her chest as the wheels of Wesley's car skidded to a halt outside of the hospital. They had no idea what they would find when they got there, but they knew they had to stop Cole before he hurt anyone else.

It was dark now. A sliver of moonlight shone through the clouds, casting a pale light over the hospital grounds. At this hour, the grounds were quiet. The only sound was the soft rustle of leaves in the breeze. The air was thick with the scent of flowers and the sound of crickets.

"Do you think he's inside or outside?" Wesley asked.

"I don't know," Taylor said. "He could be anywhere."

On the drive over, Taylor had researched more about Gary Phearson's death. It was indeed heart failure, and he'd died in the west wing of the hospital. So if Taylor had to guess where Cole might be, she'd say he was around there. But Wesley had raised a good question. Inside or outside?

"We should split up," Taylor said. "You go inside, check the west wing, see if there are any security cameras or anyone who's seen him. I'll go look around the outside of the building."

"Be careful."

"I'll find you when I'm done," she said.

Wesley nodded, and then he took off.

Taylor pulled her shirt over her shoulder so that the gun was in plain view. She held the gun in her hand, feeling its weight. She took a deep breath and then stepped outside of the car.

***

Wesley pushed through the hospital doors, the white lights piercing his eyes, and dashed for the wing Cole Phearson's father had died in. Wesley had never been a big fan of hospitals, but then again, who was? They were normally not happy places, although Wesley was lucky enough to say that most of his experiences in them had just been waiting forever for the nurse to look at Maisie if she had a bad stomach bug.

He hurried up to the reception desk in the cardiac department. A young nurse looked up at him, wide-eyed.

"Can I help you?"

"Yeah, hi," Wesley said. He flashed her his badge, and her eyes went wider. "I'm looking for information about someone who might have been visiting this wing not long ago. Cole Phearson—Gary Phearson's son."

Recognition crossed the girl's brows. "Oh, I remember Gary… we lost him a few weeks ago. It was quite sad; he was curmudgeonly, but we'd all grown to care for him."

"And Cole?" Wesley asked, his pulse in his throat.

"If you mean the boy who would visit him sometimes, then yes, I think his name was Cole. He really didn't speak, ever, actually. Gary told us he was mute."

"Have you seen him around here since Gary passed away?" Wesley asked.

"Cole?" The nurse's brows pinched. "Well, no, I don't think so. He stopped coming around after his dad died. No more reason to be here, I guess."

Wesley paused, taking it in. So, if Cole was here, he hadn't been seen—at least not in this section. His head was reeling, and he took a step back to consider what to do next. There had to be a security room around here, and he figured his next best option was to find one of the security guards and question him.

As Wesley was about to walk away, a voice drifted from around the corner. It sounded like two girls talking, whispering to each other, but he made out one sentence: "Did you see him? He was so creepy!"

Wesley, on instinct, turned the corner. There, he saw two young nurses leaning close to each other, talking.

"And he was carrying what?" one of them asked.

"I think it was a toy or something…"

Wesley didn't have time to waste. Badge out, he walked right up to them. The girls looked at him, shocked, as they took in the badge.

"Apologies for eavesdropping, but did you just saw you saw a man holding a toy?"

The one girl, a blonde, nodded, blue eyes filled with concern. "Maybe he's holding it for a child."

"Was it a doll?" Wesley asked. His heart was beating so loud, it pounded his eardrums.

"Yeah, it was," the blonde said. "Is everything okay?"

Wesley didn't have time to respond.

Cole was here.

And Taylor was going after him.

CHAPTER TWENTY SEVEN

Taylor was so nervous that her entire body was shaking. She was determined to find this man and take him back to the station. She was going to catch him and prove to everyone, especially herself, that she could do it.

So why did she feel so terrified?

This was no time to be afraid. This was a time to be heroic.

She started to walk around the side of the hospital, her eyes scanning the grounds, looking for anyone who seemed out of place. It was hard to tell in the darkness, but she looked for suspicious shadows, anyone who was lurking, not just in plain sight. She crept around the side of the building, and around back, a garden came into sight. The hedges were trimmed perfectly and the flowers were in full bloom. There were several benches in a circle around the garden. The benches were made of wrought iron and were delicate and intricate. The flowers in the garden were a riot of color and smelled divine. The garden was a peaceful oasis in the middle of the hospital grounds. Taylor imagined that people came out here, patients and visitors alike, to relax or get some fresh air during their stays here.

But that wasn't all Taylor saw.

She squinted as she drew closer.

There was a man standing there, hood up, facing a bench.

And then, in the distance, Taylor heard it:

"Help… me…"

It was a high-pitched, childlike voice. Terror squeezed Taylor's throat shut.

It was him.

She ran up to him at full speed, her gun drawn. "Stop and put your hands up!"

As Taylor got closer, her feet pounding the pavement, the man turned to face her, confused. He was holding a porcelain doll in his hands.

But Taylor stopped in her tracks.

That wasn't Cole at all. He was an African-American man, and he wore a perplexed expression. Taylor quickly tucked her gun away before the man could see.

"Hi?" he said. Taylor jogged up closer to him.

"I'm with the FBI," she said. "What are you doing with that?"

He held the doll up again. "Creepy, isn't it? I heard this weird voice, then I saw the doll sitting here… so I picked it up. Maybe some kid left it here?"

Taylor's blood ran cold. This man was about to have his throat slit, and he didn't even realize it. All that meant was that Taylor had gotten here just in time.

Cole was here.

Then, the voice:

"Put… her… down!"

Taylor spun around. The voice sounded like it was coming from all over the place. She faced the man.

"You need to get out of here now. I'm with the FBI—"

"I said put her down!" the voice screeched, and a young man with long brown hair came pouncing out of the bush, knife drawn.

Taylor shoved the witness away, and he dropped the doll to the ground. Its cheek smashed against the pavement and shattered. The doll's blue eyes stared up at the sky, unseeing.

"No!" Cole screamed, then he lunged at Taylor with the knife.

Taylor ducked out of the way just in time, and Cole passed her. She scrambled to her feet and drew her gun, then fired. The shot missed.

"Cole—" she started to call out, but just then, Cole came back around and thrust the knife into her gun arm.

Pain exploded in her arm. A hot, searing pain that shot through her muscles and made her whole body shudder. The gun fell from her numbed fingers.

Then Cole kicked her in the gut, and she fell backwards over the wrought iron bench. Her head hit the ground hard. She saw spots.

The whole thing happened so fast, so quickly, Taylor didn't even have time to think.

"You killed Betty!" Cole screamed. "You killed her! Now I'm going to kill you!" He raised the knife up high, aiming for her neck. His voice sounded like a child's—but it belonged to a monster.

Taylor rolled out of the way just in time, and the knife went flying into the rosebush. She scrambled back to her feet. Her gun was lost somewhere in the foliage.

She'd have to do this hand-to-hand.

But her gun arm was dead. She tried to move it and a lance of pain shot all the way up to her shoulder. She hissed. Her adrenaline was pumping. She was alive, and she was going to stay that way.

Cole came at her again, knife in hand. He thrust it toward her, but she was ready this time. She sidestepped out of the way and grabbed his wrist with her good hand. She twisted it hard and he yelped in pain as the knife fell to the ground.

She wasted no time. She brought her knee up into his stomach and he doubled over, gasping for air. As he did, she brought her elbow down onto the back of his neck, knocking him down. But another jolt of pain throbbed through her as her wound continued to bleed. Her head was growing light, and for a moment, Taylor was dizzy.

She looked over to see Cole charging her again with the knife. She dodged, but this time, she was woozy. What was happening? He'd just stabbed her arm, but Taylor was losing blood at an alarming rate.

Maybe he'd struck an artery.

Maybe she'd bleed to death out here.

But no. She had to stay alive. For Wesley. For herself. For everyone.

She had to save them all.

She managed to hit Cole again, but he wasn't giving up yet. He was determined to finish her off.

She didn't have time to think about it. She dodged another blow, then brought her knee up, aiming for his solar plexus. She hit him, and he dropped to the ground. He gagged, clutching his stomach.

He wasn't down for long. Cole scrambled to his feet again and came at her with a speed that Taylor didn't know was possible. He kicked her hard in the stomach, then grabbed her neck and threw her to the ground, hard. She hit the pavement back first, a terrible pain shooting up her spine. Her vision blurred again. She tried to focus on Cole, but he was nothing but a blur.

"You should've just let Betty go!" he roared. He grabbed the knife from the ground and held it high, aiming for her throat. Taylor held her arm up and the knife stabbed right into it, blocking a fatal blow. But more pain rocketed through her.

"Hey!" she heard a voice call. Taylor looked up.

Wesley came barreling around the corner, gun drawn. He didn't stop running until he grabbed Cole and shoved him to the ground. He pinned Cole down with his knee. "You don't want to do this, son," he said.

Cole struggled against the restraining arms of Wesley, breathing in and out heavily. "You think I don't want to do this?" he screamed. "I've been wanting to do it! I've wanted to do it since day one! I wanted to rip her throat out! I wanted to cut her all up and leave her for rats to eat!"

He snarled, his face was twisted with pent-up rage and hate. Wesley held him down with all his strength. Cole screamed and struggled harder, but Wesley didn't move. "You're not going to hurt anyone anymore. Do you understand?"

Cole went still. His chest heaved. Tears streamed from his eyes.

Taylor held her wound, blood leaking between her fingers and onto the ground. Cole stopped fighting, and Wesley flipped him over and slapped cuffs on him.

Cole's face was wet with tears. His eyes were red and swollen. He looked like a child.

Cole didn't say anything. He just stared at the sky.

The sky, with its million stars shining down on them.

Taylor's vision blurred and she felt dizzy. The world was spinning. She felt like she was going to vomit. She tried to take a step forward, but her legs wouldn't move. Then she felt herself falling. Falling through the darkness. Falling through the void. She felt like she was falling forever. Then she hit the ground.

The last thing she heard before she slipped away was Wesley yelling her name.

EPILOGUE

Taylor's eyes fluttered open to the sound of beeping machines. She was disoriented for a moment, until she realized she was in a hospital room. Her arm was bandaged and there was an IV in her hand.

She tried to sit up, but she felt weak and dizzy. Taylor blinked. Her eyes felt gritty, like she hadn't slept in days. She tried to sit up, but her head swam and she had to lie back down.

"What the—"

"Shh, it's okay," a voice said. It sounded like Wesley. "You're in the hospital. You're going to be alright."

Taylor looked around, trying to orient herself. The last thing she remembered was Cole attacking her. And then falling through the darkness.

"What happened?" she croaked out.

"Cole stabbed you," Wesley said gently. "More than once. But you're going to be okay. The doctors fixed you up."

Taylor swallowed hard, trying to wet her throat. "And Cole?"

"He's in jail," Wesley said. "He's not going to hurt anyone anymore."

Taylor let out a sigh of relief and sank back into the pillows. She was safe now.

She was safe.

Wesley's warm hand squeezed hers. Her head was fuzzy, but she could see him smiling at her. She was going to be okay.

She could breathe again.

"Thank you," she said.

"You know I'm here for you."

Taylor leaned back in the bed and looked around the room. "Is this the—"

"It's the hospital in Flyway," Wesley said. "I wanted to get you transferred to Baltimore so you could see your sister when you woke up, but they needed to get you in quick. That kid nicked one of your arteries, and you lost a lot of blood." Wesley squeezed her hand tighter. "I was worried about you."

Taylor smiled, feeling at ease. "Thanks, Wes…"

"I'm just glad you're safe," Wesley said. He brushed a strand of hair out of her face. "I was so scared I was going to lose you."

"I'm not going anywhere," Taylor said. She reached up and touched his cheek, letting her hand linger there for a moment.

Wesley turned his head and kissed her palm, his lips warm and gentle. Taylor's heart felt full. She knew in their rational minds, they wouldn't be so romantic like this, but maybe they were just caught up in the moment. But still. Taylor liked it this way. Based on the look in Wesley's eyes, he liked it too.

"Taylor, I…"

"What is it?"

Wesley looked like he was struggling with something. "I know this is going to sound crazy, but I think I'm falling too hard for this to just stay professional."

The words hung in the air for a moment as they stared at each other. Wesley look scared, like he was waiting for her to laugh at him or push him away. But all Taylor felt was a warmth spreading through her chest. She lifted her hand and cupped his cheek again, letting her thumb brush over his bottom lip.

"I feel the same way," she said softly.

Wesley's eyes lit up and he grinned, leaning in to kiss her. His lips were soft and gentle at first, but then they turned insistent as their mouths moved together. It was a desperate, searching kiss, full of want and need and emotion. And Taylor kissed him back with everything she had, pouring all of her feelings into it.

It had all happened so fast. But Taylor felt complete. She never thought she would, especially after her divorce from Ben. She never thought she'd fall for anybody ever again.

But here she was, falling for Wesley, and falling hard. It scared her. But it was also an amazing feeling to know somebody wanted her again.

Not just her body, but her mind and her heart as well.

He paused, pulling away slightly. "Is this okay?"

Taylor took a breath, then kissed him again. "I want to try," she said. "See where this goes."

Wesley smiled and kissed her again, longer and deeper this time. Taylor's heart raced. She realized this was the start of her new life. Without Ben. She had a good partner, and Angie was finally home.

Everything was going to be okay.

Not long ago, Taylor never would have believed she'd find happiness again. Especially with Ben. Especially due to her fertility issues. For a long time, she'd felt worthless, like all she was good for was solving cases—she even messed that up sometimes. But in that moment, Taylor felt like things really were going to work out.

When they finally pulled apart, they were both breathless. Wesley pulled her into his arms, his strong chest surrounding her. She felt tears spring to her eyes, but they were happy tears. Wesley was here, and she was in his arms. Safe. She was safe.

Just then, Taylor's phone, which was on the table beside the hospital bed, rang. Wesley grabbed it and passed it to her, and Taylor's pulse jumped at the name on the screen. It was her dad.

"Dad?" she answered.

"Taylor," her dad said. "Angie's awake."

***

Taylor burst through the doors at the Baltimore hospital. The Flyway hospital had wanted to keep her there for a bit longer, but Taylor had checked out the moment she learned Angie was awake.

Now, her feet clacked against the tile as she hurried up to Angie's room. The tile was cold and hard under her feet, and the sound echoed through the hallway. The walk seemed to go on forever, and Taylor's anxiety was through the roof.

Dr. Abrams was standing outside with a clipboard. When he saw Taylor, he stood at attention.

"I need to see her," Taylor said.

"Taylor, wait," Dr. Abrams said. "I have to warn you, you might not like what you find."

"I don't care," Taylor said, stepping up to him. "Angie's awake and I need to see her. I'll be careful."

But before Taylor could go inside, the door opened and Taylor's parents came out. Taylor's mom had clearly just stopped crying, and her eyes were red and swollen. Tears were still clinging to her eyelashes, and her makeup was smeared. Taylor's dad looked just as torn up. His eyes were bloodshot, and he was twisting a tissue in his hand.

"Mom, Dad?" Taylor asked. "What's going on?"

"Angie's awake," her mom said. "But she's not...she's not herself."

Taylor's stomach dropped. "What do you mean?"

"She's not awake...not really," her mom said. "She woke up, but she's... she's not really there. The doctors don't know what's wrong with her."

No. Taylor's nightmare was coming to life in front of her eyes. She thought back to Belasco's tarot reading. How she'd said somebody she loved might betray her. Well, that person wasn't Wesley. And it definitely wasn't her parents.

Sometimes, the tarot cards weren't literal. They were mystical in their predictions. Maybe what they'd meant was that Taylor's feelings would be betrayed by a person she loved. Maybe it meant that she'd betray herself by getting her hopes up. It could have meant anything.

All she knew was that she wouldn't believe it until she saw it. Taylor had done everything right. She'd tracked down her sister and saved her. She'd risked her own life to do it and had won.

It couldn't be over now. Taylor refused to believe it.

"I have to see her," Taylor said.

"Taylor, we don't think it's a good idea," Taylor's dad said. If he was saying that, Taylor knew it must be serious, but Taylor couldn't accept that.

Taylor's mom sniffled. "They said you'd probably be traumatized. Angie's not the same, Taylor. She's in there, but not in there. It's hard to explain."

Taylor's chest clenched. "I have to see her."

Taylor's parents exchanged a glance. Her dad nodded, and her mom let out a shuddering breath. "Be careful," she said, stepping aside.

Taylor reached the door to Angie's room and opened it, then stepped inside.

Angie was lying in the bed, her eyes closed. She looked pale and fragile, but she was alive. And right now that was all that mattered to Taylor.

"Angie," she said softly, moving closer to the bed.

Angie's eyes fluttered open and she turned her head toward Taylor. A smile spread across her face when she saw her.

But then it fell away.

"You..."

Taylor smiled. "Angie? It's me, Taylor," she said, moving closer to the bed. "Your sister."

But Angie just shook her head. "No, you... you took him from me..."

"What?" Taylor's nerves were on fire. Her eyes watered. "Took who, Angie? What are you saying?"

Angie's face twisted in anger. "You killed him!" she suddenly yelled, her voice becoming more shrill. "I loved him, and you took him away!"

Taylor couldn't believe what she was hearing. This was worse than anything she could have imagined.

Surely, Angie wasn't saying that she loved the man who'd kidnapped her for twenty years?

"You bitch!" Angie yelled. "How dare you show your face here! Go away!"

"I just want to help you!" Taylor cried. She tried to reach out, but Angie slapped her hand away.

"Help me?" Angie screamed. "You're the reason I ended up in that room!"

"No!" Taylor said. "I'm not the reason! It was him, he took you away!"

Taylor was crying now. She couldn't believe this was happening. Angie was saying these awful things, but it didn't make sense. She had to be in shock or something.

Angie crossed her frail arms over her chest. "I'll never forgive you," she said. "I'll never forget."

Taylor's lungs burned. She could hardly breathe. "But I love you," she said, tears streaming down her face. "You're my sister. I saved you. I—"

"No!" Angie shrieked. "No, you did this! You brought this on yourself! You did this! You're nothing but a murderer!"

Taylor's heart was pounding in her ears. She felt like she couldn't breathe. She stumbled back, away from the bed.

"Angie, please," she said. "I'm sorry. Please don't say those things."

But Angie was shaking her head. "I hate you, I hate you, I hate you!" she cried, and Taylor's ears were ringing. Her chest felt like it was going to burst.

"I'll never forgive you," Angie said again. Her face twisted as she looked at Taylor. "You'll never be close to me again. I'll never, never forgive you."

"I'm sorry, Angie, I'm so sorry. I want to help you. I want to help us. I'm your sister, Taylor. Don't you remember me?"

Angie just shook her head. "You're not my sister. I don't have a sister. I only have him. And you took him!" She screamed the last sentence at the top of her lungs.

The nurses ran in and quickly sedated Angie. As they were restraining her, she continued to scream and thrash about, her eyes wild with anger and hatred. "You did this!" she shouted at Taylor. "You took him away from me! I'll never forgive you! Never!" Her body was writhing and her voice was hoarse from shouting. The nurses were gentle but firm as they injected her with the sedative. Within seconds, she was unconscious.

Taylor couldn't take it anymore. She backed out of the room, ignoring her parents approaching her, then turned and ran down the hall. She couldn't stop crying, couldn't breathe.

She burst through the double doors and started running. Her shoes slapped against the linoleum floor, echoing in the empty hallway. It was almost dark when she ran outside and reached her car. Then she was driving so fast she wondered if she'd get pulled over. She didn't care. She couldn't feel anything anymore. Her hands were shaking on the steering wheel and her vision was blurred by tears.

She had to get away from this. From everything.

She pulled into the driveway and burst inside her parents' home—her childhood home. It was dark, and she couldn't see anything. But she didn't care. She stumbled up the stairs.

Her throat felt like it was on fire. She was gasping now, trying to get air into her lungs.

She ran to the room Angie used to sleep in. The door was slightly ajar, and the handle felt cool and smooth under her fingertips. She pushed it open and was enveloped in the scent of Angie's perfume. The room was exactly as it had been left. The bed was unmade, and clothes were strewn about. Posters of boy bands adorned the walls. It was as if Angie had just stepped out for a moment and would be back any second. Tears welled up in her eyes. Taylor collapsed to her knees and pressed her hand against her sister's mattress.

It was cold and abandoned, like Angie's heart. Taylor stood up again. The picture was small, but it was framed nicely. It was a picture of her and Taylor on the nightstand. They were both smiling brightly and their cheeks were rosy. They were hugging each other tightly, like happy sisters. The background was a blur, but it looked like they were at a party. They were both wearing dresses and their hair was done up nicely. Taylor was wearing a necklace with a heart pendant. Angie was wearing hoop earrings. They looked like they were having the time of their lives.

She picked the picture up and looked at it.

They were so happy when they were teenagers.

She was happy then, too.

The picture slipped from her hand and the glass shattered on the hardwood floor.

Her body shook as she fell to her knees, sobbing.

She was going to be sick.

She leaned over and retched up the contents of her stomach.

She closed her eyes, but she could still see Angie's face. She could feel her sister's words burning inside her.

She looked at the framed photo and saw what she'd done.

She'd broken it.

Just like she'd broken everything else.

She'd saved Angie's life, but this wasn't the sister she knew. She'd been too late.

The years of abuse had taken their toll. Angie had Stockholm syndrome.

And Taylor wasn't her savior. In her mind, she was her captor.

There was no other way to look at it. Angie would never forgive her. And Taylor would never forgive herself.

She'd failed her sister.

She'd failed everyone.

Taylor leaned over and retched again. It was all her fault. Everything that had happened was her fault.

She thought of her sister and the life she could have. She thought of her parents and the pain they would feel if Angie died. She thought of the people who loved her and whom she loved.

And she found the strength to stand.

Taylor had come so far. She couldn't just give up. She couldn't do it again. She couldn't watch Angie die before her eyes.

There had to be hope. There had to be. She couldn't let her sister's heart be frozen over forever.

Taylor had saved Angie physically. Now, she had to save her mentally.

There had to be a way.

Taylor wouldn't stop fighting until she found it.

NOW AVAILABLE!

<u>DON'T TELL</u>
(A Taylor Sage FBI Suspense Thriller—Book 6)

Taylor's new case takes a startlingly personal turn as she realizes the killer knows all about her personal life—and is mirroring his murders to target her. As the crime scenes inch uncomfortably close to him, Taylor must wonder—will she herself be the next victim?

"Molly Black has written a taut thriller that will keep you on the edge of your seat… I absolutely loved this book and can't wait to read the next book in the series!"
—Reader review for Girl One: Murder

DON'T TELL is book #6 of a brand-new series by critically acclaimed and #1 bestselling mystery and suspense author Molly Black.

When even her tarot reader gets stumped, Taylor knows she is in uncharted waters. Her job, and possibly her life, are on the line. All she needs to do is get inside the killer's head—before he can get inside hers.

But what if she's too late?

A page-turning and harrowing crime thriller featuring a brilliant and tortured FBI agent, the TAYLOR SAGE series is a riveting mystery, packed with non-stop action, suspense, twists and turns, revelations, and driven by a breakneck pace that will keep you flipping pages late into the night. Fans of Rachel Caine, Teresa Driscoll and Robert Dugoni are sure to fall in love.

Future books in this series will be available soon!

"I binge read this book. It hooked me in and didn't stop till the last few pages… I look forward to reading more!"
—Reader review for Found You

"I loved this book! Fast-paced plot, great characters and interesting insights into investigating cold cases. I can't wait to read the next book!"
—Reader review for Girl One: Murder

"Very good book… You will feel like you are right there looking for the kidnapper! I know I will be reading more in this series!"
—Reader review for Girl One: Murder

"This is a very well written book and holds your interest from page 1… Definitely looking forward to reading the next one in the series, and hopefully others as well!"
—Reader review for Girl One: Murder

"Wow, I cannot wait for the next in this series. Starts with a bang and just keeps going."
—Reader review for Girl One: Murder

"Well written book with a great plot, one that will keep you up at night. A page turner!"
—Reader review for Girl One: Murder

"A great suspense that keeps you reading… can't wait for the next in this series!"
—Reader review for Found You

"Sooo soo good! There are a few unforeseen twists… I binge read this like I binge watch Netflix. It just sucks you in."
—Reader review for Found You

Molly Black

Bestselling author Molly Black is author of the MAYA GRAY FBI suspense thriller series, comprising nine books (and counting); of the RYLIE WOLF FBI suspense thriller series, comprising six books (and counting); of the TAYLOR SAGE FBI suspense thriller series, comprising six books (and counting); and of the KATIE WINTER FBI suspense thriller series, comprising nine books (and counting).

An avid reader and lifelong fan of the mystery and thriller genres, Molly loves to hear from you, so please feel free to visit www.mollyblackauthor.com to learn more and stay in touch.

BOOKS BY MOLLY BLACK

MAYA GRAY MYSTERY SERIES
GIRL ONE: MURDER (Book #1)
GIRL TWO: TAKEN (Book #2)
GIRL THREE: TRAPPED (Book #3)
GIRL FOUR: LURED (Book #4)
GIRL FIVE: BOUND (Book #5)
GIRL SIX: FORSAKEN (Book #6)
GIRL SEVEN: CRAVED (Book #7)
GIRL EIGHT: HUNTED (Book #8)
GIRL NINE: GONE (Book #9)

RYLIE WOLF FBI SUSPENSE THRILLER
FOUND YOU (Book #1)
CAUGHT YOU (Book #2)
SEE YOU (Book #3)
WANT YOU (Book #4)
TAKE YOU (Book #5)
DARE YOU (Book #6)

TAYLOR SAGE FBI SUSPENSE THRILLER
DON'T LOOK (Book #1)
DON'T BREATHE (Book #2)
DON'T RUN (Book #3)
DON'T FLINCH (Book #4)
DON'T REMEMBER (Book #5)
DON'T TELL (Book #6)

KATIE WINTER FBI SUSPENSE THRILLER
SAVE ME (Book #1)
REACH ME (Book #2)
HIDE ME (Book #3)
BELIEVE ME (Book #4)
HELP ME (Book #5)
FORGET ME (Book #6)
HOLD ME (Book #7)
PROTECT ME (Book #8)

REMEMBER ME (Book #9)

www.ingramcontent.com/pod-product-compliance
Lightning Source LLC
Chambersburg PA
CBHW030613310726
48979CB00003B/702

* 9 7 8 1 0 9 4 3 9 5 4 6 3 *